雅典文化

生活句型
萬用手冊

EVERYDAY ENGLISH CONVERSATION
GUIDE

IT CAN MAKE YOU FEEL GREAT ABOUT SPEAKING ENGLISH.

MP3

國家圖書館出版品預行編目資料

生活句型萬用手冊 / 張瑜凌編著

-- 二版 -- 新北市：雅典文化，民109.05

面； 公分 -- (行動學習；16)

ISBN 978-986-98710-3-7(平裝附光碟片)

1. 英語　2. 句法

805. 169　　　　　　　　　　　　109003420

行動學習系列 16

生活句型萬用手冊

編著／張瑜凌

內文排版／鄭孝儀

封面設計／林鈺恆

法律顧問：方圓法律事務所／涂成樞律師

總經銷：永續圖書有限公司　　CVS代理／美璟文化有限公司

永續圖書線上購物網　　　　TEL：(02) 2723-9968
www.foreverbooks.com.tw　　FAX：(02) 2723-9668

出版日／2020年05月

雅典文化

出版社　22103　新北市汐止區大同路三段194號9樓之1

TEL　(02) 8647-3663

FAX　(02) 8647-3660

【前言】

學習英文的小撇步：每天開口大聲念英文

許多人都曾有過以下的疑問：

「該如何學好英文呢？」

「背了很多單字，但是遇到需要開口說英文時，就會腦袋一片空白！」

「我只想要學生活實用的英文，該如何下手呢？」

以上這些學習英文時所產生的疑問，都面臨同一個現象：缺乏情境需求的「反應式會話」練習。

隨口就能說 Thank you

何謂「反應式會話」？從老老少少都能朗朗上口地說："Thank you"或是"Sorry"就知道，因為這是屬於最基本的萬用語句，只要常聽、多練習，就能把握說英文的時機。學好英文是不分年紀的，記住兩個學習的原則，「常開口、常練習」，人人都會說英文。

精選重點句型＋超實用會話語句

「生活句型萬用手冊」收錄最常見的各種生活情境單元，利用精選重點句型＋超實用會話語句的內容，提供您自我訓練，加強「反應式會話」的口語能力。想要學好英文沒有捷徑，只要秉持「每天開口大聲念英文」的精神，你就可以脫口而出說英文。

全冊內容均外籍教師錄音導讀

本書還提供真人外籍教師錄音導讀MP3，完全收錄「生活句型萬用手冊」的所有內容，讓您能夠自行斟酌時間，利用MP3做一對一的隨讀練習，創造您無時無刻、隨口說英文的會話能力！

自
錄

MP3 001

● 瞭解事情真相

I see.

我了解。

> "see"也是動詞「看見」的意思，"I see"
> 則表示你對對方的所言已經全盤瞭解的意
> 思。

A：That's the reason why I have to call her.

那就是為什麼我應該要打電話給她的理
由。

B：Oh, I see.

喔！我瞭解了。

同義用法

例 I understand.
我了解。

例 I got it.
我了解。

例 I got you.
我懂你的意思。

例 I know what you meant.
我了解你的意思。

● 明白對方的意思
Say no more.

不要再說了。

當你已經瞭解對方的意思,也希望對方不要再滔滔不休時,就可以說"Say no more",表示「我明白了,你就不要再說了」。

A : I saw your wife went to see a movie with Kenny.

我看見你太太和肯尼去看電影。

B : Say no more.

不要再說了。

● 不明白對方的想法
I still don't get it!

我還是不明白!

當對方費盡力氣解釋後,你仍然一知半解時,就可以再次聲明:"I don't get it!"句子中的 get 表示「瞭解」的意思。

A : Is that clear to you?

這樣你清楚了嗎?

B : Sorry, I still don't get it!

抱歉,我還是不明白!

類似用法

例 I don't see the point.
我不明白。

例 I don't get the picture.
我不明白。

例 I don't understand.
我不明白。

例 I can't figure it out.
我不明白。

例 I don't know what you are talking about.
我不知道你在説什麼。

 004

● 無法理解
I didn't catch you.
我沒有聽懂！

不瞭解對方的所言除了"I don't get it!"之外，也可以說："I didn't catch you."字面意思是「我沒有跟上你」，也就是「我沒有聽懂！」的意思。

A：So we've decided to finish it by five o'clock.
所以我們已經決定五點鐘之前要完成！

B：Sorry, I didn't catch you.
抱歉，我沒有聽懂！

類似用法

🄐 I don't understand.
我不懂！

🄐 I don't get it.
我不懂！

🄐 What do you mean by that?
你這是什麼意思？

MP3 005

● 被誤解
You are missing my point.
你沒弄懂我的意思。

> 若是對方誤解你的本意時，就應該捍衛自己的想法，大膽地說出"You are missing my point."，意思是「你誤會我的重點了」。

A: Do you mean so we can climb over the fence?

你是說我們可以爬過籬笆？

B: You are missing my point. It's you, not we.
你沒弄懂我的意思，是「你」，不是「我們」！

類似用法

🄐 You don't get it.
你沒弄懂。

🄐 It's not what I meant.
我不是這個意思。

例 That's not right.
　　不對！

🎵 006

● 正確解讀
You are right.
你是對的。

當對方的想法和你一致或是你認同對方
的言論時，就可以說"You are right."

A：I think Susan is so hot.
　　我覺得蘇珊是個辣妹。
B：You are right.
　　你說對了。

類似用法

例 You are absolutely right.
　　你絕對是正確的。

例 You can say that again.
　　你說對了。

例 Now you are really talking!
　　這才像人話嘛！

例 You got it.
　　你說得對！

例 Exactly.
　　完全正確！

反義用法

例 Not exactly.
不完全正確！

● 沒聽清楚

What did you just say?

你剛剛說什麼？

沒聽清楚對方說的話時，就可以問"What did you just say?"通常用過去式的時態表示。

A：You scared the shit out of me.

你嚇得我尿失禁。

B：What did you just say?

你剛剛說什麼？

A：I said you scared me.

你說你嚇壞我了。

類似用法

例 Excuse me?
你說什麼？

例 I can't believe what you just said.
我真不敢相信你剛剛說的話！

例 Don't ever say that again.
不要再這麼說了！

MP3 008

● 請求對方再說一遍
I beg your pardon!

你說什麼？

> 因為沒聽清楚對方說的話，希望對方能再說一遍時，就可以說"I beg your pardon!"或是直接說"Pardon?"

A：Get the hell out of here!

滾開！

B：I beg your pardon!

你說什麼？

A：I said I don't want to see you anymore.

我說我不要再見到你了。

類似用法

例 Pardon?
你說什麼？

例 Excuse me?
你說什麼？

例 What did you just say?
你剛剛說什麼？

例 Come again?
你說什麼？

● 詢問意見

What do you say?

你覺得如何呢？

> "What do you say?"的字面意思雖然是
> 「你說什麼」，但另一種解讀是指「你的意
> 見是什麼」的意思。

A：I think Susan is a nice girl. What do you say?

我覺得蘇珊是個好女孩！你覺得呢？

B：Susan? Don't you think she is too young?

蘇珊？你不覺得她太年輕嗎？

類似用法

例 What do you think?
你覺得如何？

例 What do you think of it?
你覺得它如何呢？

例 What would you recommend?
你有什麼建議？

● 詢問想法

What's on your mind?

你在想什麼呢？

> 從"What's on your mind?"的字面意思判
> 斷，可以直接解釋為「你的腦袋瓜在想什
> 麼」的意思。

A：Hey, buddy, what's on your mind?

嘿，老兄，你心裡在想什麼？

B：I was wondering why she called me last night.

我在想昨晚她為什麼打電話給我。

A：Come on, just let her go, OK?

不要這樣！忘了她吧，好嗎？

類似用法

例 What are you thinking about?
你在想什麼？

例 What are you thinking of?
你在想什麼？

 011

● 附帶詢問

And you?

你呢？

當你已經問過第一個人問題，接下來要問第二個或第三個人相同的問題時，就可以直接說"And you?"

A：I'd like a cup of black tea.

我要點一杯紅茶。

B：OK. A cup of black tea. And you, sir?

好的，一杯紅茶。先生，那您呢？

C：Coffee, please.

請給我咖啡。

同義用法

例 How about you?
你呢？

類似用法

例 How about you, Mr. Black?
布來克先生，你呢？

例 How about yourself?
你自己呢？

MP3 012

● 詢問其他人的需求
Anyone else?

還有其他人要嗎？

和上一句類似，"Anyone else?"表示還有
其他人有相同的問題或需求嗎？

A：May I have another piece of apple pie?

我可以再來一片蘋果派嗎？

B：Sure. Anyone else?

好的。還有其他人要(蘋果派)嗎？

C：No, thanks.

不用了，謝謝！

相關用法

例 Anything else?
還有其他事嗎？

例 Something else?
還有其他東西？

例 Is that all?

就這樣嗎？

MP3 013

● 祝好運

Good luck.

祝你好運！

"Good luck"是一種祝福的言詞，舉凡對方需要好運氣，例如要比賽、考試等，都可以說"Good luck"表示「祝你好運」！

A：I'm going to take the written test tomorrow.

我明天就要參加筆試了。

B：Good luck, Joseph.

約瑟夫，祝你好運！

A：Thanks. I really need it.

謝謝，我真的需要（好運氣）。

類似用法

例 Wish you good luck.

祝你好運。

相關用法

例 Good luck to you.

祝你好運。

例 Good luck, buddy.

兄弟，祝你好運。

例 Good luck, kids.

孩子們，祝你們好運！

例 For good luck.
　是要祝你好運！

> A：Here you are.
> 　給你。
> B：What is this?
> 　這是什麼？
> A：My ring. For good luck.
> 　這是我的戒指。（送你）是要祝你好運！

 014

● 祝玩得愉快
Enjoy yourself!
祝你玩得開心！

> 當你聽到對方要出發去度假、遊玩、參加聚會派對等，你就可告訴對方："Enjoy yourself!"（好好玩吧！）

A：Bye, mom.
　媽咪，再見囉！
B：Enjoy yourself, son!
　兒子，祝你玩得開心喔！

同義用法

例 Have fun!
　祝你玩得開心！

相關用法

例 I really enjoyed myself.
　我玩得很開心。

> A：How is the party?
> 　　派對好玩嗎？
> B：I really enjoyed myself.
> 　　我玩得很開心。

MP3 015

●道賀

Congratulations!

恭喜！

> 　　當對方有喜事需要道賀時，少不了需要
> 你的"Congratulations!"請注意，"Congratu-
> lations!"要用複數形式表現。

A：Finally, I got that promotion.

　　我終於升遷了。

B：Congratulations. You deserve it.

　　恭喜。你應得的！

類似用法

例 I'm glad to hear that.

　　我很高興聽見這個消息！

例 I'm so happy for you.

　　我真為你感到高興！

例 It's good for you.

　　這對你來說是好事。

例 You deserve it.

　　你是值得的！

● 無奈遵從

Anything you say.

你説怎麼樣就怎麼樣！

> 當你不得不聽從對方的指示時，就可以
> 說"Anything you say"，但是要注意，這句
> 話也具有挑釁的意味，使用時要注意時機。

A：Don't forget to send me the sales report tomorrow.

　　不要忘記明天要把銷售報告寄給我。

B：Anything you say.

　　你説怎麼樣就怎麼樣！

類似用法

例 You are the boss.
你是老大，説了就算！

例 What can I say?
我能説什麼？

● 迫於無奈

What can I say?

我能説什麼？

> 「人在江湖身不由己」，當你無力改變現
> 況卻又憤恨不平時，似乎就只能説："What
> can I say?"表示「除了接受，我還能説什麼
> 呢？」

A : I think Tom should apologize to him.

我覺得湯姆應該向他道歉。

B : Well, what can I say?

這個嘛,我能說什麼?

相關用法

例 I don't know what to say.

我不知道該說什麼!

例 What shall I say?

我能說什麼?

例 See? Didn't I tell you so?

看吧!我不是告訴過你了嗎?

 018

● 言聽計從

You are the boss.

你說了算!

> 對於對方的言論你雖然不從,但是可能
> 礙於對方的輩份、職務可能比你高而不得
> 不從,只好說:"You are the boss."表示「你
> 最大,你說了算數!」

A : You have to finish it on time.

你要如期完成這件事。

B : Whatever you say. You are the boss.

就照你說的。你說了算!

類似用法

例 Whatever you say!
隨便你！

例 I will do whatever you say!
我會依你所說的照辦！

相關用法

例 Do as I said.
照我所說的去做！

 019

● 那又如何
Whatever!

隨你便！

當對方的言行舉止你不認同時，你乾脆採取放任不管的態度，此時你就可以說 "Whatever!"，表示「和自己無關」的意思。

A : I have no idea how to work it out.

我實在不知道該如何解決這件事。

B : Whatever! You don't care, right?

隨便吧！你不關心，對吧？

MP3 020

● 不在意

I don't care.

我不在意!

"care"是動詞「在意」的意思,反之"don't care"則是「不在意」。「毫不在意」則可以說"I don't care at all."

A：Look what you have done to her.

看看你對她做了什麼好事!

B：I don't care.

我不在意!

同義用法

例 I don't mind.
我不在意!

類似用法

例 I don't care about them.
我不在意他們。

例 I don't care at all.
我一點都不在意。

例 I don't give a shit.
我不在意。

●不要放在心上
Never mind.

沒關係！

> "Never mind"既可以表示勸人不要在意、不要放在心上的意思，也可以當成中文「算了」的放棄意味。

A：I don't think Susan likes you.

我不覺得蘇珊喜歡你。

B：Never mind. I don't like her, either.

沒關係！我也不喜歡她。

類似用法

 Forget it.

算了！

 It's nothing.

沒有什麼的！

 It doesn't matter.

沒關係！

●感謝
Thank you.

謝謝。

> "Thank you"也是學習英文非常重要的基本句型，簡簡單單的說法，卻可以充分表達感謝之意。

A：Thank you.

謝謝。

B：You're welcome.

不必客氣！

類似用法

例 Thank you so much.

非常謝謝你！

例 Thank you very much.

非常謝謝你！

例 Thanks again.

再次感謝你！

> A：That's very kind of you. Thanks again.
>
> 你真是太好了。再次感謝你！
>
> B：Don't mention it!
>
> 不必客氣。

 023

●不必客氣

Don't mention it.

不必客氣！

當對方向你道謝，你就要回應「不必客氣」，英文就叫做"Don't mention it."

A：Thank you so much. You've been very helpful.

謝謝你。你真的幫了大忙！

B：Don't mention it. What are friends for?

不必客氣。朋友就是要互相幫忙！

類似用法

例 You are welcome.
不必客氣！

> A：Thank you for all this.
> 　　這一切都要謝謝你。
> B：You are welcome.
> 　　不必客氣！

例 That's all right.
不必客氣！

例 Anytime.
不必客氣！

例 It's OK.
沒關係！

例 No problem.
沒問題的！

MP3 024

● 不被重視

Who cares!

沒人在乎啊！

> 若你不受到他人重視，就可以酸溜溜地抗議"Who cares!"，字面意思是「有誰在意？」其實是表達「沒有人在意」的意思。

A：I don't think we should do this, do we?

我覺得我們不應這麼做，對嗎？

B：So what? Who cares!

那又怎樣？沒人在乎啊！

類似用法

例 Nobody cares!
沒人在乎啦！

例 I don't give a good damn.
我才不在意！

MP3 025

● 是否有交往對象
Are you seeing someone?
你是不是有交往的對象？

> "Are you seeing someone?"可不是「正在看某人」的意思，而是問對方「是否有正在交往的對象」。

A：Judy, are you seeing someone?

茱蒂，妳是不是有交往的對象？

B：It's none of your business.

你少管閒事！

類似用法

例 Did you fall in love with someone?
你和某人在戀愛嗎？

相關用法

例 You're in love!
你戀愛了！

例 You look different.
你看起來很不一樣喔！

●是否當真

Are you serious?

你是認真的嗎？

> "serious" 是 指「嚴 肅 的」、「認 真 的」，"Are you serious?"表示對對方的言論感到不敢相信，也有「你是說真的嗎？」的意思。

A：I am going to marry Judy.

我要和茱蒂結婚了！

B：No kidding. Are you serious?

別開玩笑了！你是認真的嗎？

類似用法

例 You can't be serious!
你不是認真的吧？

例 Are you sure?
你確定嗎？

例 No kidding.
不是開玩笑的吧！

●嚴肅對待

I'm serious.

我是認真的！

> 若是對方質疑："Are you sure?"或是"Are you serious?"為了表示你決非兒戲，不妨嚴肅地捍衛你的認真態度："I'm serious."

A : Mark and I were separated.

馬克和我分居了。

B : Are you kidding me?

你是開玩笑的吧？

A : No, I'm serious.

不，我是認真的。

類似用法

例 I meant it.

我是認真的。

例 I'm not kidding.

我不是開玩笑的。

例 It's not a joke.

這不是開玩笑的！

反義用法

例 I'm kidding.

我是開玩笑的！

 028

● 是否確定

Are you sure?

你確定？

想要確定對方所言所語的正確性，以證明自己自己沒有認知錯誤，就可以說：" Are you sure about that? "

A : David told me that he broke up with her.

大衛告訴我他和她分手了！

B : Are you sure about that?

你確定嗎？

A : Of course.

當然確定。

● 不確定

I'm not sure.

我不確定。

萬一連你自己都不是這麼的有把握，不妨說："I'm not sure."或是說"Who knows"，表示「誰知道？我可不確定啊！」

A : Do you know where the bus station is?

你知道公車站在哪裡嗎？

B : Sorry, I'm not sure.

對不起，我不太清楚。

A : It's OK!

沒關係！

同義用法

例 I'm not sure about it.
我不太確定。

例 I'm not quite sure.
我不太確定。

例 I don't know for sure.
我不太清楚。

MP3 030

●開玩笑

You must be kidding.

你是在開玩笑的吧！

> 如果遇到常常在開玩笑、態度不認真的人，你也可以藉此反擊對方的言行："You must be kidding."表示「我實在是不相信啊！」

A：I got married yesterday.

我昨天結婚了。

B：You must be kidding.

你是在開玩笑的吧！

A：It's the truth.

是事實！

類似用法

例 No kidding?

不是開玩笑的吧！

例 Are you kidding me?

你在跟我開玩笑吧？

例 Is that a joke?

是開玩笑的嗎？

● 自找苦吃

You asked for it.

是你自己找罪受！

也許你曾經勸過對方，但對方仍舊不放在心上卻因此自討苦吃時，你就可以說"You asked for it."

A：I can't believe that it happened to me.

不敢相信這件事會發生在我身上。

B：You asked for it.

是你自己找罪受。

同義用法

 You are asking for it.
你自討苦吃！

相關用法

 He is asking for it.
他是自討苦吃！

● 感到驕傲

I'm proud of you.

我為你感到驕傲。

"be proud of + 某人"的句型，通常是父母或長官對晚輩的表現感到驕傲或欣慰時使用。

A : I made it, dad.

我辦到了，爸爸！

B : You did? My good boy. I'm too proud of you.

你辦到了？我的好孩子。我真為你感到驕傲。

同義用法

例 You really make me proud.

你真的讓我感到驕傲。

相關用法

例 You must be proud of yourself.

你一定為自己感到驕傲。

例 You must be very proud of your son.

你一定很以你的兒子為傲。

 033

● 感到厭煩

I'm tired of it.

我對它感到很厭煩了。

"be tired of it"的句型，表示感到厭煩、無奈的意思，卻沒有特別指明是哪些事。

A : This is too much! I'm tired of it.

這是太過份了！我對它感到很厭煩了。

B : What's wrong? I thought he was your best friend.

怎麼啦？我以為他是你的好朋友。

類似用法

例 I'm fed up with it.
我對它煩死了！

例 I'm sick of it.
我都膩了。

例 I hate this.
我恨死這一切了。

相關用法

例 I'm tired of being nice.
我對當一個老好人感到厭煩了。

例 I'm tired of helping him.
我對於要幫助他這件事感到厭煩了。

MP3 034

● 要求安靜
Be quiet.

安靜！

面對吵吵鬧鬧的情境時，就非常適合提出這個要求"Be quiet"，表示要求大家安靜一點的意思。

A：Hey, you guys, would you please be quiet?

嘿，各位，能請你們安靜下來嗎？

B：Oh, we're sorry.

喔，我們很抱歉！

類似用法

例 Shut up.
閉嘴！

例 Zip your lip!
閉嘴！

相關用法

例 You are too noisy.
你（們）太吵了！

MP3 035

● 抱歉打擾對方
I'm sorry to bother you.
很抱歉打擾你。

　　若是因為突然拜訪對方、插話等，都可以說"sorry to bother you"，以展現你的禮儀。

A：I'm sorry to bother you. Got a minute to talk?
很抱歉打擾你。有空談一談嗎？

B：Sure. What's up?
當然有啊！什麼事？

類似用法

例 Did I bother you?
我有打擾到你嗎？

相關用法

例 Don't bother your father.

不要打擾你的父親！

●感到訝異

My God.

我的天啊！

當聽到令人感到不敢相信、訝異的消息時，就可以說"Oh, my God."

A：My God.

我的天啊！

B：What happened?

發生什麼事了？

A：Did you see that?

你有看到那個東西嗎？

類似用法

例 Boy!

天啊！

例 Man!

我的天啊！

例 For God's sake.

天啊！

MP3 037

● 要求保持聯絡

Keep in touch.

保持聯絡。

"Keep in touch"字面意思是表示「保持互相接觸」，其實就是「保持聯絡」的意思，但沒有特別表示保持聯絡的方法。

A：Don't forget to keep in touch.

　　不要忘記要保持聯絡！

B：Sure. Thanks again for everything.

　　當然好！對所有的事情再次感謝你！

類似用法

例 Keep in touch with each other, OK?

　　要彼此保持聯絡，好嗎？

例 I'll be in touch!

　　我會保持聯絡的！

MP3 038

● 隨時保持電話聯絡

Call me sometime.

有空打個電話給我。

「保持聯絡」的選擇之一，就是電話聯絡，希望對方能夠"call me sometime"，表示「有空就撥電話給我」的意思。

A：Call me sometime.

　　有空打個電話給我。

B : I will.

我會的。

A : See you around.

再見囉！

類似用法

例 Call me, OK?

要打電話給我，好嗎？

例 Give me a call if you have a chance.

有機會的話，打個電話給我。

例 Give me a ring sometime.

有空打電話給我。

相關用法

例 Don't forget to write.

別忘了寫信(給我)。

 039

● 好好照顧自己
Take care of yourself.

你要好好照顧自己。

當兩人要道別時，就可以說"take care of yourself"，通常適用在以後會有好一陣子不會再見面時使用。

A : Good bye, my friend.

我的朋友，再見了！

B : Take care of yourself.

你要好好照顧自己。

A：I will.

我會的！

 040

●稍後再見

See you in a few minutes.

等會見。

> 和一般道再見不同，"See you in a few mi-nutes"是特別表示「等一會會再見面，現在先說再見」的意思。

A：See you in a few minutes.

等會見。

B：Fine. I'll be expecting you.

好的。我等你。

類似用法

例 See you then.

到時見。

 041

●勸人冷靜

Calm down.

冷靜下來。

> "calm down"是常用片語，表示「冷靜下來」的意思，當對方怒氣沖沖時，你就可以輕輕拍對方的肩膀說"Calm down, buddy."（好兄弟，冷靜一點）

A : I'm so angry about it.

　　我對這件事很生氣。

B : Calm down, pal. Don't lose your cool.

　　夥伴，冷靜下來！別失去理智。

類似用法

🗗 Cool down.

　　冷靜一下！

🗗 Keep your cool.

　　冷靜點！

🗗 Don't get excited.

　　別激動！

 042

● 勸人放輕鬆

Take it easy.

放輕鬆點！

> 勸人輕鬆點，就可以說 "take it easy"，或是勸人不要這麼緊張時，也可以說 "Relax"。

A : What happened to Mark? It's pretty late now.

　　馬克發生了什麼事？現在很晚了。

B : Take it easy. I'm sure he'll make it in time.

　　放輕鬆點！我相信他會及時趕到的。

類似用法

🗗 Easy!

　　放輕鬆！

例 Just relax.

放輕鬆！

MP3 043

● 勸人別生氣

Don't lose your cool.

別失去理智。

「失去理智」表示失去冷靜的頭腦，所以說千萬不要"lose your cool"。

A：I don't give a shit what David thinks.

我才不管大衛想什麼！

B：Hey, don't lose your cool.

嘿，別失去理智。

MP3 044

● 鼓勵

Cheer up.

高興點！

當有人沮喪、悶悶不樂時，你就有義務開導對方，此時的一句"Cheer up"就是鼓勵對方想開點、高興點的意思！

A：I trust you, Kenny. Don't worry about it.

肯尼，我相信你！不要擔心。

B：Thank you for cheering me up.

謝謝你鼓勵我。

類似用法

例 Hey, cheer up!

嘿！高興點！

例 Everything will be fine.

凡事都會沒問題的！

例 It's not the end of the world.

又不是世界末日！

● 勸人凡事看開些

Don't take it so hard.

看開一點！

凡事鑽牛角尖絕對是人生觀念的負面態度，如果凡事都"take it so hard"，就容易產生中文所謂的「得失心」太重。

A：I can't believe that she left me at all.

我不敢相信，她終究離開我了！

B：Don't take it so hard.

不要把事情看得這麼嚴重。

類似用法

例 Let it be.

就讓它過去吧！

● 勸人不必自責

No one blames you.

沒有人會責備你！

當有人犯錯而非常自責時，為了緩和氣氛甚至讓當事人不要遭受如此大的壓力，就可以安慰"No one blames you"，表示「沒有人責備你，你也不用如此自責了！

A：My mistake. I'm really sorry about it.

我的錯！我真的很抱歉。

B：No one blames you.

沒有人會責備你！

同義用法

例 Don't blame yourself.

不要自責！

相關用法

例 It's not your fault.

這不是你的錯！

MP3 047

● 勸人不必擔心

Don't worry.

不用擔心！

同樣是一句經典、實用的句子，當有人
顯得憂心忡忡時，拍拍對方肩膀，勸勸對
方"Don't worry" 吧！

A：Why did you go to see the movie with that guy?

你為什麼要和那傢伙去看電影？

B：Don't worry. I am a big girl.

不用擔心！我已經是個大人了。

(說話者是女性)

類似用法

例 Don't worry about it.
不要擔心它。

例 Don't let that worry you.
別讓那事折磨你了。

例 Try not to worry.
試著不要擔心!

 048

● 擔心

I am so worried.

我真的很擔心。

為了表達你的擔心與不安,你可以說"I'm so worried",反之,若是沒有什麼好擔心的,就可以說"Nothing worries me"表示沒有任何事足以讓我擔心!

A : I am so worried.
我真的很擔心。

B : Come on, nothing is happening.
別這樣,沒事的!

類似用法

例 But I am so worried about him.
但是我真的很替他擔心。

MP3 049

● 要求單獨相處

Can I get you alone?

我能不能跟你單獨相處一會兒?

"alone"是副詞「單獨地」的意思,若是希望能和一群中的某一人單獨相處,以避開其他閒雜人等,就可以說:"Can I get you alone?"

A：What is the matter with you?

你發生了什麼事?

B：Can I get you alone?

我能不能跟你單獨相處一會兒?

A：Of course. What's up?

好啊!什麼事?

類似用法

例 Can I get you a second?

我可以佔用你一點時間嗎?

例 Can I speak to you in private?

我可以私底下和你談一談嗎?

MP3 050

● 想要和對方談話

Got a minute to talk?

有空談一談嗎?

想要和對方談話的問句非常多種,"Got a minute to talk?"是最常見的,或是直接簡單地問:" Got a minute?" 對方就會瞭解你想談話的要求。

A: Got a minute to talk, Mr. White?

懷特先生,有空談一談嗎?

B: Sure. Have a seat.

當然有!坐吧!

同義用法

例 Got a minute?

有沒有一點時間 (談幾句話)?

例 Can I talk to you now?

我現在可以和你說句話嗎?

例 Can I talk to you for a moment?

我能和你說說話嗎?

 051

●不會耽擱太久

It won't keep you long.

不會耽誤你太久。

若是因為有事相求或希望佔用對方一點時間,為了讓對方知道這件事不會花太多的時間,不會造成對方的困擾,就可以說:"It won't keep you long."讓對方安心。

A: Can I talk to you? It won't keep you long.

我能和您談一談嗎?不會耽誤你太久。

B: Sure. What's up?

當然可以。有什麼事嗎?

類似用法

例 It won't be long.
不會耽擱太久的。

例 It won't take you long.
不會花你太久的時間。

例 I'll make it quick.
很快的就會好的！

反義用法

例 Sorry, I took so long.
抱歉，耽擱這麼久！

 052

● 改變話題

Let's change the subject.

我們換個話題吧！

當大家在聊天時，卻觸碰了你不願意提及的話題時，就可以說："Let's change the subject."讓其他人知道你不願提及這個敏感話題也無妨。

A：I don't think he is your Mr. Right.

我不認為他是你的真命天子。

B：Let's change the subject.

我們換個話題吧！

類似用法

例 I don't want to talk about it.
我不想討論這件事。

例 Let's stop talking.

不要再說了！

例 Let's talk about it later.

晚一點再聊吧！

MP3 053

● 尋求幫助

I need your help.

我需要你的協助。

若是需要幫忙，請不用客氣直接說出來。只要不是太過份的要求，大部分的人會願意伸出援手的。

A：I need your help.

我需要你的協助。

B：What is it?

什麼事？

同義用法

例 Could you give me a hand?

你能幫我一個忙嗎？

例 Would you do me a favor?

您能幫我一個忙嗎？

例 Can you help me with this?

可以幫我這個忙嗎？

類似用法

例 Give me a hand!

幫幫我！

例 Do me a favor.

幫我一個忙。

> A：Do me a favor.
> 　幫我一個忙。
> B：Sure. What can I do for you?
> 　好啊！我能幫你什麼？

 054

●詢問是否需要幫助
May I help you?

有什麼需要我效勞的嗎？

> 當你看見有人似乎需要幫助，但對方又沒有主動提出要求時，此時你就可以問問對方："May I help you?"或是"What can I do for you?"

A：May I help you?

有什麼需要我效勞的嗎？

B：Yes. Please hold this for me.

有的！請幫我拿著。

類似用法

例 Do you need any help?
你需要幫助嗎？

例 What can I do for you?
我能為你做什麼？

例 How can I help you?
我要怎麼幫你？

● 主動提供幫助

Let me help you.

我來幫你。

主動協助人是一種美德，像是看見孕婦搬重物或行動不便者要上車時，都應該主動說："Let me help you."

A : It looks heavy. Let me help you.

看起來很重耶！我來幫你。

B : Thank you for your help.

謝謝你的幫助！

類似用法

例 Let me help you with this.

這個讓我來幫你吧！

例 Let me give you a hand.

我來幫你吧！

例 Just let me know if you need any help.

如果你還需要其他幫助，讓我知道一下！

例 Please let me know if there's anything I can do for you.

有什麼是我可以幫你做的，讓我知道一下！

🎧 056

●答應提供幫助

What do you want me to do?

你想要我做什麼？

> 當對方提出要求希望你能協助時，你可以主動問問對方需要何種協助："**What do you want me to do?**"，表示「有什麼要我做的？」

A：Please do me a favor.

請幫我一個忙。

B：Sure. What do you want me to do?

好啊！你想要我做什麼？

類似用法

例 Is there anything I can do for you?

有什麼需要我幫你做的嗎？

相關用法

例 Can I get a taxi for you?

需要我幫你叫一輛計程車嗎？

> A：Can I get a taxi for you?
>
> 需要我幫你叫一輛計程車嗎？
>
> B：Yes, please.
>
> 好的，謝謝！

● 接受對方的幫忙

Thank you for your help.

感謝你的協助囉!

> 和一般感謝的 "Thank you" 不同,在此是特別針對對方提供協助的道謝。

A : Would you like me to take this for you?

你想讓我幫你拿嗎?

B : Yes. It's very kind of you.

好的!你真好。

類似用法

例 Thank you for your help.

感謝你的協助囉!

例 Wouldn't that be too much bother?

那不是太麻煩你了嗎?

● 謝謝好意

No. Thanks.

不用了,謝謝!

> 若是對方主動表達願意幫忙的意願,而你實在是可以自行處理,不需要對方的協助,還是記得要向對方說聲謝謝!

A : Is there anything I can do for you?

有什麼需要我幫你做的嗎?

B : No. Thanks.

不用了,謝謝!

生活句型
萬用手冊

MP3 059

● 拒絕對方的幫忙

Please don't bother.

請不必這麼麻煩。

> "No. Thanks."是拒絕對方協助後感謝的用法，而"Please don't bother."則強調「自己不願意麻煩對方」的方式，以回絕對方的協助！

A：Anything I can buy for you?

需要我幫你買什麼嗎？

B：Please don't bother.

請不必這麼麻煩。

同義用法

例 Don't bother.

不必麻煩！

類似用法

例 Please don't bother. Thank you all the same.

不用麻煩你了！還是得謝謝你。

●有能力自己處理

I can manage it by myself.

我可以自己處理。

> 回絕對方的協助，是因為自己可以自行處理，那麼就讓對方知道你不是因為客氣才不接受幫助，而是因為"I can manage it by myself."

A：Madam, allow me.

女士，讓我來吧！

B：Don't bother. I can manage it by myself.

不必麻煩！我可以自己處理。

同義用法

例 I can handle this by myself.

我可以自己處理。

例 I can take care of it by myself.

我可以自己處理這件事。

類似用法

例 I am OK.

我可以自己處理！

例 I am all right.

我沒事的！

例 Don't worry about me.

不要擔心我。

MP3 061

● 仰賴他人
I'm counting on you.

萬事拜託了!

> 當你仰賴某人當你的左右手處理大小事時,那麼就應該讓對方知道"I'm really counting on you."表示「我的確是凡事都靠你」!

A : I'm counting on you, Susan. Please don't quit.

蘇珊,我很依賴妳的。請不要辭職!

B : But I have to. I've already found a new job.

但是我一定要。我已經找到新工作了!

類似用法

例 I count on you.
我很依賴你。

例 We are counting on you to solve it.
我們依賴你來解決這件事。

例 I can't live without you.
沒有你我活不下去!

例 I can't do that without you.
沒有你我辦不到!

●別寄予希望

Don't count on me.

別指望我。

"count on" 表示「仰賴」、「依靠」的意思，否定用法就表示「別指望我」或「我不值得你依賴」的意思。

A：Nobody knows.

沒有人會知道！

B：Kenny? How about you?

肯尼？你呢？

C：Don't count on me.

別指望我。

反義用法

例 I count on you.

萬事拜託了！

A：Can I count on you to be there for me?

我能仰賴你幫我去那裡嗎？

B：I'll do my best.

我會盡力！

類似用法

例 Don't look at me.

別看我！

063

● 詢問是否說得夠清楚

Do I make myself clear?

我說得夠清楚了嗎?

當你發表言論後,為了確保對方都瞭解你的意思,甚至是強調你的堅定立場時,都可以說:"Do I make myself clear?"表示「我說得夠清楚了吧?不要誤解我的意思!」

A：I won't let it happen in my class. Do I make myself clear?

我決不允許這件事在我的班上發生。我說得夠清楚了嗎?

B：Yes, sir.

是的,老師。

類似用法

例 Didn't I make myself clear?

我說得還不夠清楚嗎?

例 Is that clear?

夠清楚嗎?

例 Have you got it?

明白了嗎?

例 Do you hear me?

有聽見嗎?

> A : Do you hear me?
> 你有聽懂嗎？
> B : Yes, mom.
> 有的，媽咪！

● 被嘲笑

They always make fun of me.

他們老是嘲笑我。

> "make fun of +某人"表示嘲笑、戲弄某人的意思，和"laugh at"的意思是一樣的。

A : I don't want to go out with them.

　　我不想和他們一起出去。

B : Why not?

　　為什麼不想？

A : Because they always make fun of me.

　　因為他們老是嘲笑我。

類似用法

例 Don't laugh at me.

　別嘲笑我！

例 Don't make fun of me.

　不要嘲笑我！

例 Don't tease me.

　別嘲笑我！

例 Get off my back!

不要嘲笑我！

例 You teased me.

你在嘲笑我。

🎵 065

●沒有面子
Shame on you!

你真丟臉！

當有人做了某事是不被允許、甚至不道德的、會令人蒙羞的事件時，就可以告誡對方：**"Shame on you!"** 表示「你真是丟臉啊！」

A：Shame on you. You never take the kids to the park.

你真丟臉。你從不帶孩子們去公園玩。

B：I have been busy. You know that.

我一直很忙。你是知道的。

同義用法

例 It's shame on you.

你太丟臉了。

類似用法

例 You're a disgrace.

你真丟臉！

例 How could you do that?
你怎麼能這麼做？

例 Look at yourself.
瞧瞧你自己這付德行！

MP3 066

● 提議開車接送

Let me drive you home.

讓我開車載你回家。

> 如果你願意開車送朋友回家，只要用動詞"drive"（開車）即可，就叫做"drive + 某人 + home"。

A：What's the rush?
你趕著要去哪裡？

B：I have to be home before three o'clock.
我要在三點鐘前到家。

A：Don't worry. Let me drive you home.
不用擔心！讓我載你回家。

類似用法

例 Do you need me to drive you home?
你需不需要我載你回家啊？

例 I can drive you home.
我可以送你回家。

例 Wanna lift?
要搭便車嗎？

MP3 067

● 提出接送的要求

Can you give me a lift?

可以開車送我回家嗎？

"give me a lift"也是常用片語，表示「順路搭便車」的意思，例如："I can give you a lift."

A：Can you give me a lift?

可以開車送我回家嗎？

B：Sure. Get in.

當然好！上車吧！

類似用法

例 He asked me for a ride into town.

他要求搭我的便車進城！

MP3 068

● 向異性表白

I'm falling in love with you.

我愛上你了！

「表白」是男女之間發展戀情的第一步，如何向對方表白又不會肉麻呢？可以試著用這句"I'm falling in love with you."表示「我愛上你了！」

A : Stop calling me! It really bothers me.

不要再打電話給我了。這讓我很困擾！

B : But I can't help it. I'm falling in love with you.

可是我情不自禁。我愛上你了。

類似用法

例 I love you.
我愛你！

例 I miss you.
我想你。

例 I'm crazy for you!
我為你瘋狂！

例 I'm drawn to you.
我被你深深吸引。

例 I fell for you at first sight.
我對你一見鍾情。

例 You look great.
你看起來好漂亮。

> A : How do I look?
> 我看起來如何？
> B : You look great.
> 你看起來好漂亮。

MP3 069

● 少吹牛了
Give me a break.

別吹牛了！

如果有人老是喜歡誇大、吹牛，下次當他又在吹牛時，你就可以說："Give me a break"，表示「少吹牛了，我不相信」的意思。

A：I was invited to sing a song on TV.

我受邀在電視上唱歌。

B：Come on, give me a break. I don't buy it.

得了吧，少來了！我不相信！

類似用法

例 Come on.

你少扯了吧！

例 Get out!

少來了！

MP3 070

● 別來這套
Come on!

少來了！

這句"Come on!"可以適用在很多情境當中，例如要對方「別來這套」時、邀請對方一起加入、請對方動作快一點…等，都可以說："Come on!"

A：I don't wanna go with you.

我不想和你一起去。

B：Come on, honey, don't we have a deal?

不要這樣嘛，親愛的！我們不是已經有共
識了嗎？

類似用法

例 I don't believe it.

我才不相信。

例 I don't want this.

我也不想要這樣！

> A：It's getting worse. Kenny.
>
> 肯尼，情況越來越糟了耶！
>
> B：I don't want this.
>
> 我也不想要這樣！

MP3 071

● 催促對方快一點

Hurry up!

快一點！

> 催促對方「動作加快」除了上述的"Come
> on!"之外，也可以說"Hurry up!"或"Quickly"
> 等。

A：Hurry up, or we'll be late.

快一點，不然我們就要遲到了。

B：It's still early.

還很早啊！

類似用法

例 Hurry!
快一點！

例 Quick!
快一點！

例 Come on, move on.
快一點，動作加快！

MP3 072

● 打賭

I bet.

我敢打賭！

當一群人在自吹自擂時，某個人甚至會撂下一句自信的話"I bet"，表示他對自己的言論很有把握！

A：I'm going to ask her out.

我要約她出去。

B：I don't think you could make it. I bet.

我不這麼認為你辦得到！我敢打賭。

A：Why not?

為什麼辦不到？

相關用法

例 I bet you'll have to pay for it.
我敢說你一定會為此事付出代價。

● 視情況決定

It depends.

看情況再說！

許多事情並不是黑白分明般清晰，介在 yes 或 no(也是也不是)這種模擬兩可的情境中非常常見，此時你的回答可以用"It depends"來回應，表示事情仍舊有變化，要視情況而定。

A：What are you going to do?

你打算怎麼作？

B：I have no idea. It depends on the situation.

我不知道。要視情況而定。

類似用法

例 We'll see.

再說吧！

例 Could be, but I'm not so sure.

有可能，但是我不是很確定。

● 受夠了

Enough!

夠了！

enough 是指「夠了的」意思，除此之外，也可以用"Enough!"表示喝令住手、不要再說的意思，另外，還含有「我受夠了」、「不耐煩」的意思。

A：Enough! I will punish both of you.

夠了，我兩個人都要處罰！

B：But he bit me too.

但是他也有咬我。

類似用法

例 It's enough.

夠了。

例 Stop it.

住手！

例 Don't do this anymore.

不要再這麼做了！

MP3 075

● 喝令停止動作

Stop it.

住手！

> 除了"Enough!"之外，也可以用"Stop!"表達「喝令停止」的目的，更具有權威性要求對方停止一切動作的喝阻作用。

A：Stop it, you guys!

你們快住手！

B：What? We did nothing.

什麼？我們什麼都沒有做！

● 請對方讓路

Excuse me.

借過！

中文的「借過」在英文中並沒有相對應的翻譯名詞，但可以用"Excuse me"達到相同的效果，表示「借過」、「抱歉打擾」的意思。此外，若是兩人正在說話時，你突然要接電話，也可以說："Excuse me."

A：Excuse me.

借過！

B：Sure.

好啊！

● 暫時離席

Will you excuse us?

請容我們先離席好嗎？

上述的"Excuse me"是表達個人的歉意，若用"Excuse us"則通常表示兩人以上要在談話團體中（例如用餐時）暫時離席的意思。

A：Will you excuse us?

請容我們先離席好嗎？

B：Sure. Go ahead.

好啊！去吧！

MP3 078

● 好主意
It's a good idea.

好主意！

> 當對方提出一個不錯的想法或建議，並得到你的認同時，你就可以用 "good idea" 支持對方提出的言論。

A：Why don't we try the Chinese food?

我們何不試試中國料理？

B：It's a good idea.

好主意！

類似用法

例 Great idea!

好主意！

例 Sounds good.

聽起來不錯！

相關用法

例 Interesting.

有趣喔！

079

● 見怪不怪

It happens.

常有的事。

> 某人發現了一件離奇事件，但對你來說，這是「見怪不怪」，也就是這件事經常發生，實在不足為奇時，因為「沒什麼大不了」，就可以說'It happens."

A：Look! He is so weird. What is he doing out there?

瞧！他好奇怪。他在那裡做什麼？

B：It happens.

常有的事。

類似用法

例 It happens all the time.

常有的事！

例 It's no big deal.

這沒什麼大不了！

080

● 隨口的問候

How are you doing?

你好嗎？

> "How are you doing?"是一句非常口語化的問候語，適用在非正式場合，問候的雙方也是屬於非常熟識的朋友。

A：Good morning, Paul.

　　保羅，早安！

B：Good morning, Kenny. How are you do-ing?

　　早安啊，肯尼。你好嗎？

A：Pretty good. And you?

　　我很好！你呢？

類似用法

例 How do you do?

　　你好嗎？

例 How are you?

　　你好嗎？

> A：Hi, Peggy! Come on in and sit down.
>
> 　　嗨，佩姬！進來坐！
>
> B：Hi, George. How are you this evening?
>
> 　　嗨，喬治！你今晚好嗎？
>
> A：Good. How about you?
>
> 　　很好！妳呢？

 081

● 晨昏問候

Good morning.

早安。

　晨昏的問候是最基本的打招呼的方式，
一句簡單的"Good morning"問候，可是會融
化彼此的冷漠距離感喔！

A : Hello, Henry. It's Tracy.

喂，亨利，我是崔西。

B : Hello, Tracy. Good morning.

喂，崔西，早安。

相關用法

例 Good afternoon.
午安。

例 Good evening.
晚安。

（晚上剛見面時的打招呼方式）

例 Good night.
晚安。

（晚上要道別時的打招呼方式）

> A : I have got to go to bed.
> 我要去睡覺了！
> B : OK. Good night.
> 好的！晚安。

MP3 082

● 問候不在場的第三者

How is your father?

你父親好嗎？

"How are you"是和對方招呼兼問候的語
句，若是要問候第三人，則只要換掉主詞
對象及相對應的動詞即可，例如："How is
your sister?"（你姊姊好嗎？）

A : Hi, John. How have you been?

嗨，約翰，你好嗎？

B : Great. Thanks. How is your father?

不錯！謝謝關心！你父親好嗎？

 083

●好久不見

Long time no see.

真是好久不見了。

假如突然遇見好久不見的朋友時，就可以說"Long time no see"，和中文的架構是不是很類似呢？

A : Hi, David.

嗨，大衛！

B : John! Long time no see.

約翰！真是好久不見了。

類似用法

 I haven't seen you for ages.

真是好久不見了。

 084

●意外的偶遇

I never thought that I'd see you here.

沒想到會在這裡遇見你。

若是在路上突然和某位熟識的人不期而遇，就可以說"I never thought that I'd see you here." 或是"What a coincidence." 表示「好巧啊！」

A：David? Is that you?

　　大衛？是你嗎？

B：Hi, Susan, I never thought that I'd see you here.

　　嗨，蘇珊，沒想到會在這裡遇見妳。

 085

●有一段時間未曾見面

I haven't seen you for a long time.

我好久沒見到你了。

> 若是已經有一段時間未曾再見過面，除了"Long time no see"之外，也可以說"I haven't seen you for a long time"。for 的後面可以加上時間的長短，例如好幾天、好幾個星期、好幾年等。

A：I haven't seen you for a long time.

　　我好久沒見到你了。

B：Yeah, it's been a long time, hasn't it?

　　是啊！真的是好久了，不是嗎？

相關用法

例 I haven't seen you in years.
　　好幾年不見了。

例 I haven't seen you for months.
　　好幾個月沒見到你了。

例 I haven't seen you for weeks.
　　我好幾個星期沒見到你了。

MP3 086

● 這陣子都去哪兒

Where have you been?

你都到哪兒去了？

和某個人失聯好一陣子後，再遇見對方時，就可以用完成式句型說："**Where have you been?**"表示「這陣子你人都到哪兒去了？」

A：John? I can't believe it. It's been a long time.

約翰？不敢相信！好久不見了！

B：David! Where have you been?

大衛！你都到哪兒去了？

MP3 087

● 關心對方的近況

How's it been going?

近來如何？

想要知道對方的近況時，就可以關心對方："**How's it been going?**"表示想要瞭解對方的近況。

A：How's it been going, Kenny?

肯尼，近來好嗎？

B：Not very well. I got divorced last month.

不太順利，我上個月離婚了。

A : Sorry to hear that.

很遺憾聽見那件事。

相關用法

例 What's new?

近來有什麼新鮮事？

MP3 088

●今天過得如何
How was your day?

你今天過得如何？

適用在常常見面的熟識人之間，可能早上才見過面的鄰居，晚上再見面時，就可以關心對方："How was your day?"（今天過得如何？）

A : How was your day, Kenny?

肯尼，你今天過得如何？

B : My day went pretty well. How about you?

我今天過得很好。你呢？

A : Horrible. I didn't finish my report in time.

可怕！我沒有如期完成我的報告！

相關用法

例 How was school today?

今天在學校過得如何？

例 How was work?

(今天)工作順利嗎？

🎵 089

● 是否順利

How did it go?

事情順利吧？

當你知道對方最近正在忙某一件事時，就可以隨口問問事情是否順利："How did it go?"

A：How did it go, Susan?

蘇珊，事情還順利吧？

B：Everything went well. And you?

一切都順利。你呢？

A：Terrible. I just had a car accident last week.

糟透了！我上星期出車禍了。

類似用法

例 How is everything?

凡事都順利吧？

例 Is everything all right?

凡事都好吧？

🎵 090

● 找工作

I'm looking for a job.

我正在找工作。

"look for a job"是慣用片語，表示「找工作」的意思。"look for"是「尋找」的意思，不論具體或非具體事物皆適用。

A：Anything new?

最近有什麼事嗎？

B：I'm looking for a job.

我正在找工作。

MP3 091

● 對方的氣色很差
You look rather pale today.

你今天臉色看起來很蒼白。

　若是對方看起來臉色明顯很蒼白，就應該關心對方的身體狀況："You look rather pale."順便問問他："Are you OK?"

A：Hello, David. You look rather pale today. Are you OK?

你好，大衛。你今天臉色看起來很蒼白。你沒事吧？

B：I feel sick.

我覺得不舒服。

類似用法

例 You look awful.
你看起來遭透了！

例 You look terrible.
你看起來糟透了！

MP3 092

● 生病了

I've got a fever.

我發燒了。

「生病」的表達方式有很多種，例如常見的"I am sick"（我生病了）或是"I've got a fever"（我發燒了）都適用。

A：You look awful.

你看起來糟透了！

B：I've got a fever.

我發燒了。

類似用法

例 I've got a headache.
我頭痛。

例 I've got a stomachache.
我胃痛。

例 I've got a sore throat.
我喉嚨痛。

例 I've got a running nose.
我流鼻水。

例 I've got a bad cough.
我咳嗽得厲害。

例 I can't stop coughing.
我不停地咳嗽。

例 I can't stop sneezing.
我不停地打噴嚏。

● 身體不舒服

I ache all over.

我渾身都在痛。

若是沒有生病，但就是渾身痠痛，就可以用"I ache all over"表達。"all over"是「全身上下」的意思。

A：Are you OK? You look very tired.

你還好吧？你看起來很累耶！

B：I ache all over.

我渾身都在痛。

相關用法

例 I can't eat.

我吃不下。

● 身體微恙

I'm not feeling well now.

我現在身體不太舒服。

通常表示有點不舒服的情況，但沒有特別說明是否有生病。"feel well"表示感「覺狀況很好」的慣用語句。

A：I'm not feeling well now. I don't think I can go to the party tonight.

我現在身體不太舒服。我看今晚的派對我無法參加了。

B : Oh, dear. I'm sorry to hear that.

哎呀！這太遺憾了。

MP3 095

●關心生病的朋友
How are you feeling today?

你今天感覺怎麼樣？

> 朋友生病正在復原休息中，除了問"Are you OK?"之外，也可以問："How are you feeling today?"以瞭解一下對方的復原進度。

A : How are you feeling today? Are you all right?

你今天感覺怎麼樣？還好吧？

B : I'm OK, except that I've got a bad cough.

還好，只是還一直在咳嗽。

類似用法

例 How are you feeling now?
你現在感覺如何？

相關用法

例 Feel better soon.
祝你早日康復。

例 I hope he is OK.
希望他恢復得不錯！

> A : Please say hi to him for me, OK? I hope he is OK.
>
> 請代我向他問好，好嗎？希望他恢復得不錯！
>
> B : It's very kind of you to say so.
>
> 感謝你的關心。

 096

●是否無恙

Are you OK?

你還好吧？

萬用語句"Are you OK?"適用在非常多的情境中，例如對方生病了、不對勁、心事重重、表現失常…等，一句"Are you OK?"能讓對方感受你付出的關懷。

A : It hurts.

好痛！

B : Are you OK?

你還好吧？

類似用法

⑩ Are you alright?

你還好吧？

⑩ Are you sure you are OK?

你確定你沒事？

097

● 聽聞某些消息

I heard about what happened to you.

我聽説了發生在你身上的事。

消息的流通是非常迅速的，當你聽聞某人的消息時，就可以主動告知你的關心，以表達你的慰問之情。

A：I heard about what happened to you.

我聽説了發生在你身上的事。

B：You did?

是嗎？

 098

● 從未聽説過

That's news to me.

沒聽過這回事！

當你聽見一件從未聽過的消息時，為了表示你從未知道這個消息或是這是個令人訝異的消息時，就可以說："That's news to me."

A：This is not good for you.

這對你不好啊！

B：That's news to me.

沒聽過這回事！

（例） That's news.

沒聽過這回事！

（例） Never heard of that!

沒聽説過！

MP3 099

● 過得好嗎？

What's up?

近來好嗎？

> "What's up?"不但適用在口語對話中的隨意問候，也適用類似在線上聊天室和對方打招呼的情境中，表示「近來好嗎？」或是「有什麼事？」的意思。

A：What's up?

近來好嗎？

B：Not much. I have really been busy with school.

沒什麼特別的事！我學校的事還是很忙。

（例） Anything new?

近來如何？

> A：Anything new?
> 近來如何？
> B：Nothing special.
> 沒什麼特別的事！

MP3 100

● 過得不錯

Fine, thank you.

很好,謝謝你。

當對方問候你的近況時(例如"How are you?"),你得禮貌性地回應對方的關心,此時就適合回答"Fine, thank you.",表示「謝謝關心」的意思。

A: Hello. How are you?

嗨!你好嗎?

B: Fine, thank you. How about you?

很好,謝謝你。你呢?

A: Not bad, thanks.

還不錯,謝了。

MP3 101

● 最近忙於工作

Just really busy with work.

工作真的很忙!

若有人關心你的近況,你可以說"busy with work",表示最近真的是忙於工作。with 後面可以接所忙的事。

A: How have you been?

近來好嗎?

B: Great. Just really busy with work.

很好!工作真的很忙!

●不順利

I'm not myself today.

我今天什麼事都不對勁！

> 每天面對不同挑戰的工作，難免會有挫折或不順遂的時候，此時你就可以說"not myself today"，表示「一切都不對勁」！

A：You look terrible. What's wrong?

你看起來糟透了！怎麼啦？

B：I don't know. I'm not myself today.

我不知道，我今天什麼事都不對勁！

同義用法

例 I was having a bad day.

我今天做什麼事都不太對勁。

 103

●狀況不好

Not so good.

沒有那麼好！

> 既然是"not so good"（沒那麼好），就表示狀況不太順利，甚至是很糟糕的意思。

A：How is business?

生意如何？

B：Not so good.

不是很好！

類似用法

例 Not as good as usual.
不像平常那麼好！

例 Not as good as you thought.
沒有像你想像中的這麼好！

例 So far so good.
還過得去。

例 So-so.
馬馬虎虎。

MP3 104

● 安然無事

Nothing is happening.

沒什麼大事！

「沒有消息就是好消息」，所以沒什麼事
發生（Nothing is happening）就表示日子
過得還可以。

A：You look terrible. What's going on?
你看起來糟透了！發生了什麼事？

B：Nothing is happening.
沒什麼大事！

類似用法

例 Nothing much.
沒什麼！

例 I'm OK.
我很好！

例 Don't worry about me.
別擔心我！

MP3 105

●沒有太大改變
Same as always.
還是老樣子！

中文常說的「老樣子」就是"same as al-
ways"，表示和以往差不多。要注意，當你
回答"same as always"時，對方必須是熟知
你以往狀況的人，而不是面對一個剛認識
的人的回答。

A：How are you doing, Kenny?
肯尼，近來好嗎？
B：You know, same as always.
你知道的，還是老樣子！

同義用法

例 The same as usual!
一如既往！

例 Still the same.
老樣子。

MP3 106

●介紹新朋友認識
I'd like you to meet my friend.

我想讓你來認識一下我的朋友。

希望你的兩位朋友透過你互相認識，就可以告訴他們"meet my friend"，表示「來見見我的朋友」。

A：I'd like you to meet my friend David.

我想讓你來認識一下我的朋友大衛。

B：David? You mean Susan's husband?

大衛？你是指蘇珊的先生嗎？

類似用法

 I'd like to introduce my friend David.

我來介紹一下我的朋友大衛。

 Let me introduce my friend David to you.

讓我把我的朋友大衛介紹給你。

MP3 107

●介紹雙方認識
Chris, this is Jane.

克里斯，這是珍。

介紹朋友們互相認識，必須先介紹雙方的名字，通常用"this is + 名字"的句型，表示「這是某人」的意思。

A : Jane, this is Chris. Chris, this is Jane, my sister.

珍，這是克里斯。克里斯，這是我妹妹珍。

B : Nice to meet you.

很高興認識你。

C : Nice to meet you, too.

我也很高興認識你。

類似用法

例 Meet David.

來見一下大衛。

例 Come to see my roommate.

來認識一下我的室友。

 108

● 初認識的問候

I'm pleased to meet you.

我很高興認識你。

> 認識新朋友時，萬用句型的問候絕對適用："How do you do?"另一方就可以回答："Great. You?"表示「我很好，你好嗎？」

A : How do you do?

你好。

B : I'm pleased to meet you.

我很高興認識你。

同義用法

例 Glad to meet you.
很高興認識你。

 109

● 認識新朋友
Nice to meet you.
很高興認識你。

當新朋友問候你："My pleasure to meet you."（認識你是我的榮幸），你就可以回答："Nice to meet you, too."（我也很高興認識你）

A：This is my wife Jane. Jane, this is David.
這是我太太，珍。珍，這是大衛。
B：Nice to meet you, Jane.
很高興認識妳，珍。
C：Nice to meet you, too.
我也很高興認識你。

類似用法

例 My pleasure to meet you, David.
大衛，很高興認識你！

●向新朋友自我介紹

Hello, my name is David.

你好,我叫做大衛。

> 若沒有透介紹而認識的新朋友,則可以主動告知對方自己的名字:"my name is + 名字"主動釋出善意。

A:Hello, my name is David.

你好,我的名字叫大衛。

B:Hi, I am Susan.

你好,我是蘇珊。

類似用法

例 I'm David.

我叫大衛。

例 I'm John, by the way.

對了,我叫約翰。

> A:Lovely weather, isn't it?
> 天氣很好,不是嗎?
> B:Yeah, it is.
> 是啊!的確是的!
> A:I'm John, by the way.
> 對了,我叫約翰。
> B:Nice to meet you, John.
> 約翰,很高興認識你。

MP3 111

●久仰大名
I've heard a lot about you.

久仰大名！

> 當你和新朋友間有共同認識的朋友時，就非常適合說：**"I've heard a lot about you."** 表示中文的「久仰大名」，意即「我們的共同朋友常常談論起你」的意思！

A：I've heard a lot about you. Kenny told me so much about you.

久仰大名！肯尼告訴我好多有關你的事。

B：Really? Was it good or bad?

真的啊？都聽說了什麼好事還是壞事？

同義用法

例 I've heard so much about you.

久仰大名！

> A：I've heard so much about you.
> 我已經久仰你的大名了。
> B：Same with me. By the way, how are things going with you?
> 我也是。順便問一下，你現在好嗎？

● 遇到面熟的人
You look familiar.

你看起來很眼熟！

> 若是路上巧遇看起來很面熟的人，你就可以告訴對方："You look familiar."表示「你看起來很眼熟，好像我們認識的樣子」！

A：You look familiar.

你看起來很眼熟！

B：David? It's me, Susan.

大衛嗎？是我，蘇珊啊！

113

● 長得很像某人
You look like somebody.

你看起來好像某個人。

> 表示對方和你認識的某個人長得很像的意思。

A：Do I know you?

我認識你嗎？

B：I don't think so.

不認識吧！

A：You know, you look like somebody.

你知道嗎？你看起來好像某個人。

MP3 114

●以前是否見過面
Have we ever met before?

我們以前見過面嗎？

若是你不確定眼前的人是否自己認識，就可以試探性地問對方："Have we ever met before?"再由對方的回答來判斷彼此是否認識。

A：Have we ever met before?

我們以前見過面嗎？

B：I don't think so.

沒有吧！

類似用法

例 Have we met before?

我們以前認識嗎？

MP3 115

●是否認識某人
Do you know Susan?

你認識蘇珊嗎？

若是不確定彼此是否有共同的朋友，也可以問問對方："Do you know + 人名?"

A：David, do you know Susan?

大衛，你認識蘇珊嗎？

B：I don't believe we've ever met before.

我想我們以前沒見過面吧！

●確認兩人沒見過面

I don't think you've met each other before.

我想你們倆以前沒見過面吧！

要介紹兩位朋友彼此認識時，可以利用「兩人都沒有見過面」的理由促使彼此認識："Have you ever met before?"（你們倆以前見過嗎？）

A：I don't think you've met each other before. Susan, meet my friend David. David, this is Susan.

我想你們倆以前沒見過吧！蘇珊，來見我的朋友大衛。大衛，這是蘇珊。

B：Glad to meet you.

很高興認識你。

C：Nice to meet you, too.

我也很高興認識你。

●與某人是否熟識

Are you familiar with Mr. Smith?

你和史密斯先生很熟悉嗎？

不但要知道對方是否認識某人，更要知道對方與他是否熟識的情境時，就可以問問："Are you familiar with + 人名?"

A：Are you familiar with Mr. Smith?

你和史密斯先生很熟悉嗎？

B：No, I am not.

沒有，完全不認識！

MP3 118

● 介紹常提及的朋友

David is the guy I was telling you about.

大衛就是我常常向你提起的那個人。

告訴要彼此認識的其中一人，「這個人就是我常常向你提起的人」，也讓被提及的人知道你常常聊起他。

A：He looks familiar.

他看起來很眼熟！

B：David is the guy I was telling you about.

大衛就是我常常向你提起的那個人。

A：David Smith?

就是大衛・史密斯？

MP3 119

● 閒談間提及天氣

What a lovely day!

天氣真是好呀！

「天氣」永遠是開啟話匣子的好話題，就像台灣人常常隨口問「吃飽沒？」是一樣的。"What a + 天氣型態"表示對天氣的閒聊。

A：What a lovely day!

　天氣真是好呀！

B：Yes, isn't it?

　是啊，可不是嗎？

類似用法

例 It's a nice day, isn't it?

　今天天氣不錯呀，不是嗎？

例 It's a bit cloudy, isn't it?

　今天有點多雲，不是嗎？

例 It's rather windy today.

　今天的風真大。

例 It's bitterly cold today.

　今天特別冷。

例 It's snowing heavily.

　雪下得很大。

MP3 120

● 某個日子快到了

Summer is around the corner.

夏天快要到了。

> "be around the corner"表示某個日子快要來臨了，例如四季、節慶…等都適用。

A：Hello, Bill. How are you today?

　嗨！比爾，今天好嗎？

B：Fine, thanks. Beautiful day!

　我很好，謝謝。今天天氣真好！

A：Yes. Summer is around the corner.

是呀，夏天快要到了。

MP3 121

● 詢問時間

What time is it?

幾點了？

詢問「現在幾點鐘」的萬用句型："What time is it?"

A：What time is it?

幾點了？

B：Sorry. My watch seems to be slow.

抱歉。我的錶好像慢了。

A：It's OK.

沒關係！

類似用法

例 What's the time?

幾點了？

例 What time do you have?

你知道幾點了嗎？

例 Have you got the time?

你知道幾點了嗎？

例 Could you tell me the time?

你能告訴我幾點了嗎？

● 鐘錶時間是否準確
Is your watch right?

你的錶準嗎？

中文的「準時」在英文中並沒有相對應的翻譯，英文的「是否準確」的問法只要用"Is your watch right?"表示「你的錶正確嗎？」也就是「是否準時」的問句。

A：Is your watch right?

你的錶準嗎？

B：It gains thirty seconds a day.

它每天快三十秒。

相關用法

例 It keeps good time.

這錶走得很準。

例 It loses about two minutes a day.

它每天慢兩分鐘。

> A：Does your watch keep good time?
>
> 你的錶時間準確嗎？
>
> B：It loses about two minutes a day.
>
> 它每天慢兩分鐘。

MP3 123

● 説明時間

It's seven o'clock sharp.

七點整。

> 說明「現在幾點鐘」只要用"數字+o'clock sharp"就代表「幾點整」的意思。另外，若是帶有分鐘的鐘點時間，則是"點鐘+分鐘"句型即可，例如"seven thirty"表示「七點卅分」。

A：What time is it by your watch? Mine seems to be fast.

　　你的錶幾點了？我的(錶)好像太快了！

B：It's seven o'clock sharp.

　　七點整。

類似用法

例 It's eight forty-five.
　　八點四十五分。

例 It's fifteen after three.
　　三點十五分。

 MP3 124

● 有人敲門

Who is it?

是誰啊！

> 有人敲門的時候，可千萬不要依照中文「你是誰」的邏輯思考問對方"who are you?"應該是問"Who is it?"

A：(Knock, knock, knock!)

（敲門聲）

B：Who is it?

是誰啊！

A：It's Tom.

我是湯姆。

 125

● 臨時拜訪

I'm sorry to bother you.

抱歉打擾你一下。

> 若是有事請教需要打擾對方時，就可以說"sorry to bother you"，表示「抱歉要打擾你一下！」

A：Good evening, John. I'm sorry to bother you.

約翰，晚安！抱歉打擾你一下。

B：That's OK. I was just watching television. Come in. Would you like ...uh... some coffee?

沒關係！我剛剛在看電視。進來吧！你要喝…嗯…咖啡嗎？

 126

● 招待訪客

What would you like to drink?

要喝點什麼？

> 訪客來訪時，應該要提供一些飲料給對方，此時就可以問問對方："What would you like to drink?"或是直接問對方要不要喝點水："Would you like some water?"

111

A：What would you like to drink? Coffee?

要喝點什麼？喝咖啡好嗎？

B：Yes, please.

好的，謝謝！

MP3 127

● 招呼賓客用餐

Help yourself.

別客氣，自己來！

宴客的主人告訴賓客想吃什麼盡量吃或
主動一點自己動手取食物時，就可以說：
"Help yourself."

A：Help yourself.

別客氣，自己來！

B：No, thanks. I'm full.

不用了，謝謝！我飽了。

相關用法

例 Make yourself at home.

把這裡當成自己的家。

MP3 128

● 道別

See you next time.

下次見。

中文的道別語句「下次見」，在英文也有
相同類似的話句可以使用："See you next
time."

A：It's pretty late now.

現在很晚了。

B：OK, that's it. See you next time.

是啊，就這樣囉！下次見囉！

類似用法

例 See you.
再見！

例 See you around.
再見！

例 See you soon.
再見！

例 See you later.
再見！

 129

● 剛認識時的道別

Nice meeting you.

很高興認識你！

"Nice meeting you"是慣用語句，適用在剛認識的新朋友要道別時使用，既可以是「很高興認識你！」也可以同時具有「再見」的意思。

A：Nice meeting you. Bye.

很高興認識你！再見！

B：Me too. See you.

我也是。再見囉！

🎧 130

● 等待的公車來了

Here comes my bus.

我的公車來了。

> 「我的公車來了」英文怎麼說？很簡單，
> 只要這麼想：「現在過來的就是我要搭的公
> 車」，英文就叫做"Here comes my bus."

A：Oh, excuse me, here comes my bus. Call me, OK?

噢，對不起，我的公車來了。打電話給我，好嗎？

B：I will. Bye.

我會的。再見。

A：See you soon.

再見。

🎧 131

● 質疑

Why?

為什麼？

> 當你產生疑問時，只要簡單一句"Why?"
> 就能充分傳達你的疑惑。

A：I missed the train this morning.

我今天早上錯過火車了。

B：Why? What happened?

為什麼？發生什麼事了？

例 How come?
為什麼？

例 What for?
為什麼？

MP3 132

● 令人疑惑

It's so confusing.

事情還是很令人疑惑。

> 事情的真相令人感到疑惑、不解，甚至有點是非混淆時，就可以說："It's confusing."（事情令人疑惑），但若是「我感到疑惑」，則要用"I am confused."

A：You still didn't get it, did you?

你還是沒弄懂，對嗎？

B：No, I didn't. It's so confusing.

沒有，我不懂。事情還是很令人疑惑。

類似用法

例 I doubt it.
我很懷疑！

例 It's too good to be true.
哪有這麼好的事！

例 It can't be.
怎麼可能！

● 被搞糊塗

I'm confused.

我被搞得糊里糊塗的！

> 和前面提過的"it's confusing"不同，"I'm confused."是特指「『人』被事情搞得糊里糊塗」的意思。

A：They decided to get married next month.

他們打算下個月要結婚。

B：Next month? I'm so confused.

下個月？我被搞得好迷糊了！

類似用法

例 I'm a bit confused.
我有點被搞得糊里糊塗的！

例 It's confusing.
事情令人糊塗！

例 It confused me.
我被搞得糊里糊塗的！

相關用法

例 You're confusing him!
你把他搞得糊里糊塗的。

● 分享消息

Guess what?

你猜猜怎麼了？

"Guess what?"有點類似無意識的問句，類似中文的「你知道嗎？」的用法，意在打開話匣子，後面要說明的事件，才是你要說的重點。

A：Guess what? I just passed the entrance exam.

你猜猜怎麼了，我剛剛通過入學考試了。

B：Congratulations.

恭喜你。

類似用法

🔟 You know what?
你知道嗎？

🔟 Check this out.
聽好！

🔟 Look.
聽我說！

🔟 Listen to me.
聽我說！

🎵 135

● 告知訊息

I have something to tell you.

我有事要告訴你。

有事情想要告訴對方時，可以先用"I have something to tell you."當成開場白，讓對方心裡有個準備。

A：I have something to tell you.

我有事要告訴你。

B：What's up? You look so upset.

怎麼啦？你看起來好沮喪！

🎵 136

● 直接告知

Tell me about it.

說來聽聽！

若是對方吞吞吐吐，或是故做神秘地試探你守祕密的能力，不妨直接告訴對方"Tell me about it."表示「你就直接說吧，不要拐彎抹角」。

A：Did you know what happened to us?

你知道我們發生什麼事了嗎？

B：Tell me about it.

說來聽聽！

類似用法

例 Try me.

說來聽聽！

> A : You're not going to believe it.
>   你不會相信的！
> B : Try me.
>   說來聽聽！

🎵 137

●小道消息

Have you heard about David's story?

你有聽説大衛的事了嗎？

> "Have you heard about …?"有點類似中文「你有聽説…」，非常適合在散佈消息時使用。

A : Have you heard about David's story?

你有聽説大衛的事了嗎？

B : What's wrong?

怎麼啦？

🎵 138

●聽到不好的消息

Oh, my God. Is he OK?

喔，天啊！他還好嗎？

> 當聽聞到不好的消息時，可以關心一下事件主角的現況："Is he/she OK?"表示「他/她還好吧？」

A：He had a car accident last night.

他昨晚發生車禍了！

B：Oh, my God. Is he OK?

喔，天啊！他還好嗎？

A：I don't know.

我不知道！

相關用法

例 God bless him.
願上帝保佑他！

 139

●質疑消息來源
Says who?

誰說的？

當聽見一則令人難以置信的消息時，可以追問一下消息來源的管道："Says who?"表示你想要知道「這件事是誰說的？」

A：David is going to quit.

大衛要辭職了！

B：No kidding? Says who?

真的嗎？誰說的？

A：Someone you don't know.

是你不認識的人。

● 懷疑真實性

Is that so?

真有那麼回事嗎？

> 聽到令人不敢相信的消息時，你不但訝異，更不敢相信自己的耳朵，同時亟欲確認事情的真實性時，就可以問問對方："Is that so?"

A：What kept you so late?

什麼事讓你耽擱得這麼晚？

B：I missed the train.

我錯過火車了。

A：Is that so? Liar.

是嗎？你說謊。

類似用法

例 Really?

真的？

例 Is that true?

真是事實嗎？

例 No kidding?

不是開玩笑的吧！

例 Are you telling the truth?

你說的是事實嗎？

MP3 141

●詢問原因

How come?

為什麼？

"How come?"可不是字面意思「如何過來」的意思，而是和"why"很類似，都是在問「為什麼」的意思。

A：I really dislike Susan.

我真的不喜歡蘇珊。

B：How come? I thought she was your best friend.

為什麼？我以為她是你的好朋友。

相關用法

例 Why not?

為什麼不要？

MP3 142

●受寵若驚

I'm flattered.

我受寵若驚。

當對方稱讚你或是把你捧上天時，你一定會覺得自己「受寵若驚」，英文中的「受寵若驚」就叫做"I am flattered."

A：Would you like to have dinner with me?

要和我一起共進晚餐嗎？

B：Yes, I would love to. I'm flattered by your invitation.

好啊！我願意。對於你的邀請，我感到受寵若驚。

類似用法

例 I feel flattered.
我受寵若驚。

例 I feel greatly flattered.
我真是受寵若驚。

 143

●拒絕透露訊息
I'm not telling.
我不會說的。

若是有人想向你探詢消息的來源，而你是口風非常緊的人，就可以義正嚴詞地告訴對方："I'm not telling."表示你絕對不會透露任何一丁點消息。

A：Come on, tell me the secret between you and Mark.

得了吧！告訴我你和馬克之間的秘密。

B：I'm not telling.
我不會說的。

類似用法

例 I'm not going to tell you.
我不打算告訴你。

例 I won't let you know.
我不會讓你知道！

例 No comment.
不予置評！

相關用法

例 Why shall I tell you?
我為什麼要告訴你！

MP3 144

● 並非故意
I didn't mean to.

我不是故意的。

> 當你不小心冒犯對方，不管是言行或舉止，都可以說：**"I didn't mean to."** 順便再向對方致歉：**"Please accept my apology."**

A：Hey, watch out, buddy. You stepped on me.

嘿，老兄，小心點。你踩到我了！

B：Sorry, I didn't mean to.

抱歉，我不是故意的。

相關用法

例 It's not what I meant.
那不是我的意思。

例 I didn't mean that.
我不是那個意思。

例 Sorry for that.
我為那件事抱歉啦！

● 傳達自己的本意
It's exactly what I mean.
我就是這個意思。

> 若是對方誤解你的本意，經過你的解釋後，對方才恍然大悟時，你就可以鬆一口氣：**"It's what I mean."** 表示「這才是我的意思。」

A：Are you saying that you are going to quit?
你是說你要辭職？

B：It's exactly what I mean.
我就是這個意思。

類似用法

例 I mean it.
我是認真的。

例 It's not what I mean.
我不是這個意思。

● 慎重思考
Let me see.
我想想。

> 當對方提出疑問希望你能回答或解決時，你有權要求對方先讓你想一想：**"Let me see."**

A：What do you think of it?

這件事你覺得如何？

B：Let me see. I think we should leave right now.

我想想！我覺得我們應該馬上離開！

A：Right now? Are you crazy?

現在？你瘋啦？

類似用法

例 Let me think about it.
讓我想一想。

 147

● 個人的想法
Just a thought.

只是一個想法。

> 當你發表言論後，卻又想不希望擔負太多責任時，就可以說："It's just a thought." 表示「這是我個人的想法，各位可以參考參考。」

A：What did you just say?

你剛剛說了什麼？

B：Never mind. Just a thought.

沒關係，只是一個想法。

同義用法

例 Just an idea.
只是一個想法。

例 Here is my idea.
這是我的主意。

例 Listen to this.
何不聽聽我的想法。

相關用法

例 I was wondering.
我只是在想！

 148

●不知道
I don't know.
我不知道。

> 英文中的「不知道」的說法有許多種，最常見的就是"I don't know"，可適用在正式場合，而另一種非正式場合常用的口語用法則為："I have no idea."

A : Do you know where the post office is?
你知道郵局在哪裡嗎？

B : Sorry, I don't know. I'm a stranger here myself.
對不起，我不清楚。我對這裡也不熟。

類似用法

例 I have no idea.
我不知道。

例 I don't know about it.
我不知道這件事。

例 I have no clue.
　　我不知道。

🎵 149

● 對一切一無所知
I know nothing about it.
我一無所知！

> 要特別強調你的「不知道」是「對一切都一無所知」或「沒有一丁點瞭解」時，可以說：「I know nothing about it.」

A：Who did this in my kitchen?
　　誰在我的廚房做的好事？
B：Don't look at me. I know nothing about it.
　　不要看我！我一無所知！

相關用法

例 I don't know, either.
　　我也不知道！

🎵 150

● 強調對方搞不清楚
You have no idea.
你完全不知道！

> 「You have no idea.」除了是說明對方「完全不知道」之外，也可以是質疑對方「搞不清楚狀況」的意思。

A：Why? What makes you think so?

為什麼？你為什麼要這麼做？

B：You have no idea.

你根本什麼都不知道！

MP3 151

●質疑對方沒有仔細聽
You're not listening to me.

你沒在聽我說！

> "not listen to me"除了是指對方「沒有聽我的話」，也可以抱怨對方沒有戴著耳朵仔細聽的意思。

A：What does it mean?

那是什麼意思？

B：You're not listening to me.

你沒在聽我說！

MP3 152

●詢問對方的想法
What do you mean by that?

你這是什麼意思？

> 當對方發表言論後，你可以特別針對他的所言提出質疑："What do you mean by that?"表示「你這句話這是什麼意思？」

A：Maybe David is the killer.

也許大衛就是兇手。

B：What do you mean by that?

你這是什麼意思？

A：You still don't get it, do you?

你還是不懂，對嗎？

MP3 153

● 不敢相信

I can't believe it.

真教人不敢相信！

表示你實在不敢相信聽到的消息時，就可以說："Oh, my God, I can't believe it." 不論是好事或壞事都適用。

A：I want Tom to be my boyfriend.

我要湯姆當我的男朋友。

B：I can't believe it. He doesn't like you.

真教人不敢相信！他不喜歡妳啊！

類似用法

例 I don't buy it.

我才不信這一套！

例 It's impossible.

不可能吧！

例 It can't be.

不可能的事！

例 No way.

不會吧！

例 No shit!

你少扯了！

● 不可能的事
It can't be.

不可能的事。

> 除了表示「事情不會是現在這種情境」，
> 更透露出自己不敢相信的態度。

A：Susan is about to leave.

蘇珊要離開了。

B：It can't be. She promised me to stay.

不可能。她有答應我要留下來。

類似用法

🔘 It's impossible.
不可能。

🔘 I don't think so.
我不這麼認為。

🔘 Bullshit.
胡扯！

反義用法

🔘 It's possible.
是有可能的。

🔘 Why not?
為什麼不可能？

MP3 155

●不同意
I couldn't agree less.

我是絕對不會同意的。

> 表示和對方不相同的立場或是不同意對方的所言時,你不但可以說:"I don't agree." 也可以說:"I couldn't agree less." 以強調「我是絕對不會同意的。」

A: I think it's a great opportunity.

我認為這是一個好機會。

B: I don't think so. I couldn't agree less.

我不這麼認為。我是絕對不會同意的。

類似用法

例 I don't agree with you.

我不同意你的意見。

相關用法

例 I don't agree with you on many things.

許多事情我和你持不同看法。

反義用法

例 I agree with you.

我同意你的看法。

例 I totally agree with you.

我完全同意你的看法。

例 I couldn't agree more.

我完全同意。

MP3 156

● 沒有時間

I don't have time.

我沒有時間。

中文常說「我沒有那個美國時間」表示
自己實在很忙，英文就只要說"I don't have
time."就可以了！

A：Can you walk my dog after dinner?

晚餐後你可以幫我遛狗嗎？

B：I am afraid not. I don't have time.

恐怕不行。我沒有時間。

類似用法

例 I don't have time to do it.

我沒有時間去做。

相關用法

例 Do you have time?

你有空嗎？

> A：Do you have time?
> 你有空嗎？
> B：Sure. What's up?
> 有啊！什麼事？

📀 157

● 是否在忙
Keeping busy?

在忙嗎？

"Keeping busy?"是一句精簡的問句，全文是"Are you keeping busy?"詢問對方「現在是否正在忙」的意思，通常是有求於人時使用。

A：Keeping busy?

在忙嗎？

B：No, not at all. What's up?

不，一點都不會。有什麼事嗎？

A：Can I talk to you now?

我現在可以和你說句話嗎？

類似用法

例 Busy now?

現在忙嗎？

例 David, are you busy now?

大衛，你現在在忙嗎？

📀 158

● 正在忙
I'm quite busy now.

我現在很忙。

明白地告訴對方你現在正在忙：**"I'm quite busy."**所以請對方請勿打擾或長話短說！

A：Got a minute to talk?

有空嗎談一談嗎？

B：Sorry, I'm quite busy now.

抱歉，我現在很忙。

類似用法

例 I'm in the middle of something.

我(現在)手頭上有事。

MP3 159

● 解雇

I got fired.

我被炒魷魚了。

> 「我被炒魷魚了」該怎麼說？很簡單，
> 就叫做："I got fired."另一種常見的用法是"
> be laid off"。

A：You look upset. Are you OK?

你看起來心情不好！你還好嗎？

B：I got fired.

我被炒魷魚了。

A：Oh, I'm sorry to hear that.

喔，真是遺憾。

類似用法

例 I was laid off.

我被解雇了。

例 They kicked me out.

他們把我開除了。

相關用法

例 You are fired.
你被解雇了！

MP3 160

● 人被困住

I got stuck!

我被困住了。

> 舉凡被困在車陣中、某個地方等，都可以說"I got stuck!"

A：Why were you late again this morning?
為什麼你今天早上又遲到了？

B：I got stuck in the traffic jam this morning.
今天早上我被困在車陣中動彈不得。

相關用法

例 I got stuck at the airport.
我被困在機場了。

例 I got stuck on the top of a mountain.
我被困在山頂上。

 161

● 機會極大

I guess I will.

也許我會。

> "I guess I will."是透露自己「也許會這麼做」的意思，但沒有說明是哪一件事。

A：Why don't you call her again? You still love her, don't you?

你何不再打電話給她？你依然愛著她，不是嗎？

B：I guess I will.

也許我會（打電話給她）。

類似用法

例 I guess so.
我想是吧！

例 Maybe, maybe not.
可能吧！

例 Yes, and no.
也是，也不是！

反義用法

例 It's impossible.
不可能！

 162

● 別無選擇
I have no choice.
我別無選擇。

因為別無選擇所以不得不做出超出平常會做的決定時，就可以說"I have no choice."或是"I have to."表示是被迫的及出於無奈的。

A：Why did you do that?

你為什麼這麼做？

B：Don't ask me why. I have no choice.

別問我為什麼。我別無選擇。

類似用法

例 I have no options.

我別無選擇。

例 I have no other choice.

我別無選擇。

例 There is no choice.

別無選擇。

相關用法

例 I have to.

我必須這麼做！

MP3 163

●尚未決定
I haven't decided yet.

我還沒有決定。

> "I haven't decided yet."是現在完成式，表示截至目前為止，尚未做出決定的意思。

A：Are you ready to order?

你要點餐了嗎？

B：I haven't decided yet.

我還沒有決定。

A：How about the steak? It's the specialty of the house.

要不要試試牛排？這是招牌菜。

反義用法

例 I have decided.

我已經決定了！

相關用法

例 You decide.

由你決定！

 164

● 事不關己
It's up to you.

由你決定。

> 表示決定權是在對方，對方要如何做都是"up to you"與你沒有關係，既尊重對方的決定權，也和自己擔負的責任劃清界限。

A：If it's up in the air, then I don't want to talk about it.

假使這件事尚未確定，我就不想討論這件事。

B：It's up to you. You are the boss.

由你決定！你說了就算！

類似用法

例 Up to you.

由你決定。

例 It's your own decision.
這是你自己要做的決定。

例 Make up your mind.
你作個決定吧!

MP3 165

● 期望

I hope so.

希望如此。

> 也許事情並非如期望般實現,但仍舊抱有一絲絲的期望時,就可以說"I hope so."

A：You can do your best to finish it.
你可以盡你所能去完成。

B：I hope so.
我也希望是如此。

類似用法

例 I hope you are right.
希望你是對的!

例 I guess so.
我猜也是如此。

例 I think so.
我想也是如此。

例 That's what I expect.
那是我所期望的!

●提出警告

I warned you.

我警告過你了。

> 明白告訴對方「我之前就已經警告過你，誰教你不聽我的話」時，就可以說"I warned you before."

A：I didn't expect it to happen.

我沒有預期會發生這件事。

B：I warned you yesterday.

我昨天就警告過你了。

類似用法

- 例 I told you so.

  我已經告訴過你（會發生這個情形了）。

- 例 There you are.

  看吧！我已經告訴過你。

- 例 You were not listening to me.

  你沒聽我的話！

相關用法

- 例 I've told you not to do it.

  我告訴過你不要這麼做了！

MP3 167

●盡力而為
I will do my best.

我會盡力的！

> "I will do my best."是承諾自己會盡力，也安撫對方不用擔心、全包在我身上的意思。

A：Can you finish it by 5 P.M.?

你能在五點鐘之前完成嗎？

B：I'll do my best.

我盡量。

類似用法

例 I'll try my best.
我盡量。

例 I'll try to.
我盡量。

相關用法

例 I'll see what I can do.
我來看看我能幫什麼忙！

> A：What should I do?
> 我該怎麼辦？
> B：Don't you worry about that. I'll see what I can do.
> 你別擔心！我來看看我能幫什麼忙！

●願意嘗試

I will try.

我會試試看。

> "I will try."表示請對方給自己一個機會，自己會把握機會，也願意試試看的意思。

A：Why don't you ask your parents for help?

你為什麼不向你的父母求助？

B：That's a good idea. I will try.

那是一個好主意。我會試試看。

類似用法

例 I'll take a shot.
我會試試看。

例 I'll try again.
我會再試一次！

相關用法

例 Try again.
再試試。

 169

●值得一試

It's worth a shot.

那值得一試。

> 當某件事對大家來說是冒險的、不值得一試時，你仍舊立場堅定地表示「值得一試」就可以說："It's worth a shot."

A：What do you think of my idea?

你覺得我的主意如何？

B：It's worth a shot.

那值得一試。

類似用法

📖 You'll never know what you can do until you try.

你不試試看怎麼會知道結果！

📖 Keep trying and you'll find the answer eventually.

繼續試試看，最終你會找到答案的。

MP3 170

● 確實如此

I will say.

的確是這樣。

> "I will say"的字面意思是「我會這麼說」，但背後隱藏的意思是「的確是這樣」的肯定立場。

A：I don't think Chris is Susan's style.

我覺得克里斯不是蘇珊喜歡的類型。

B：I will say.

的確是這樣的。

類似用法

📖 You are right.

沒錯！

例 That's right.
沒錯！

例 Yes, it is.
是的，的確是！

MP3 171

● 邀約來訪

You must come over to my place for dinner.

你一定要到我家來吃飯。

人際關係的維持方法之一就是憑藉聚會來維繫關係，你可以善用"come over to my place for dinner"的邀請語句，或是釋出"Please join us"的善意。

A : You must come over to my place for dinner. We have a lot to talk about.

你一定要到我家來吃飯。我們好好聊聊。

B : It sounds like a good idea.

好主意。

 MP3 172

● 邀約聚會

Let's do lunch sometime.

我們找個時間一起吃午飯吧！

朋友就是需要偶爾見面、聯絡感情，找個時間一起吃個飯是個不錯的選擇！
"do lunch"是「吃午餐」的意思。

A : Listen. Let's do lunch sometime.

聽著！我們找個時間一起吃午飯吧！

B : Sure. How about this Friday? I'll pick you up.

好啊！就這個星期五如何？我去接你！

類似用法

例 How about a drink tonight?
今晚喝一杯怎樣？

例 We need to get together sometime.
我們應該找個時間聚一聚。

 173

● 建議時間

How about this Friday?

這個星期五怎樣？

若要想提出意見給對方參考時，就可以利用"How about …"的句型。

A : When is a good time to come?

那什麼時候去好呢？

B : How about this Friday?

這個星期五怎樣？

A : That's fine with me.

我可以。

● 約定再見面的時間
See you Friday.

星期五見。

"See you"是「道別再見」的意思,若是後面再加上日期,則表示雙方約定再見面的日期。

A：See you Friday.

星期五見。

B：See you.

再見。

● 邀請參加
Would you like to join us?

你要加入我們嗎?

"join"是動詞「加入」的意思,也非常適合使用在邀請對方參加某個活動或聚會的情境使用。

A：Would you like to join us?

你要加入我們嗎?

B：Yes, I would love to.

好啊!我很樂意去。

MP3 176

●吆喝一起參加

In or out?

參加或退出?

"In or out?"是美國年輕人之間常見的用語,表示詢問對方「要加入或退出」的意思。若是願意加入,就說"I am in."

A:In or out?

你到底要不要參加?

B:OK, I will go with you.

好,我會和你一起去。

C:I'm in, too.

我也要參加。

類似用法

例 Coming or not?

到底要不要來?

例 Who is with me?

有誰要一起參加?

例 Anyone else?

還有人(要去)嗎?

MP3 177

●要求加入

Do you mind if I join you?

我可以加入你們嗎?

當你想要加入其他人的聚會、團體或談話時,可以禮貌性地問對方是否可以"join you"。

A : Do you mind if I join you?

　　我可以加入你們嗎？

B : Yes. We do mind.

　　會！我們很介意！

MP3 178

● 答應加入

Count me in.

把我算進去。

當對方問"In or out?"時，若是願意加入除
了說"I am in"之外，也可以說"Count me in."

A : Are you in or out?

　　你到底要不要參加？

B : Count me in.

　　把我算進去。

C : No, thanks.

　　不用，謝啦！

類似用法

例 I am in.

　　我也要參加。

例 Hey, count me in!

　　嘿，我要加入！

反義用法

例 I quit.

　　我退出。

MP3 179

●吆喝同行

Let's go.

我們走吧！

> 表示可以出發、或吆喝一起行動時，就可以說"Come on, let's go."

A：Come on, let's go.

快點，我們走吧！

B：But I don't want to go.

但是我不想去。

A：What happened? I thought you wanted to go.

怎麼啦？我以為你想去！

類似用法

例 Come on, hurry up.

快一點！

同義用法

例 Shall we?

可以走了嗎？

> A：Shall we?
>
> 可以走了嗎？
>
> B：Sure. Let's go.
>
> 好啊！走吧！

● 讓對方先請

After you.

您先請！

> 當要進電梯、進門或進去某個地方時，可以禮貌性地請對方先進去，就說"After you."若是你不想先進去，也可推託地說"After you."

A：You first.

您請進！

B：No. After you.

不！您先請！

● 情況越來越糟

It's getting worse.

事情越來越糟了。

> 當事情不如預期順利，甚至越來越糟糕時，就可以說"It's getting worse."有點類似中文「每況愈下」的意境。

A：How is the relationship between you guys?

你們之間的關係如何了？

B：I don't know. It's getting worse, I guess.

我不知道。我猜越來越糟了。

類似用法

例 Worse, I guess.
我想很糟!

例 It's terrible.
很糟糕!

相關用法

例 Oh, I don't think you want to know.
喔,我不認為你會想要知道!

 182

●時候到了
It's about time.

時候到了。

> "It's about time."是指「時候到了」,表示該有所行動,至於是哪件事,則彼此心知肚明。類似「時間到了」的情境也可以用"time to do +某事"來表示。

A:Come on, hurry up. It's about time.

嘿!快一點,時候到了。

B:Time for what?

是時候要做什麼?

A:Time to have dinner.

要吃晚飯了!

類似用法

例 That's it. It's about time.
就這樣!是時候了。

相關用法

例 It's about time to face the problem.
是該面對問題的時候了。

例 Time to go.
該走了！

●說來話長

It's a long story.
事情說來話長。

當事情複雜程度是必須花很多時間解釋時，而你顯得無奈、不願意說明的情況下，就可以說"It's a long story."對方就未必會勉強你做說明。

A：Tom and I broke up last month.
湯姆和我上個月分手了。

B：How come? What happened to you?
為什麼？你們怎麼啦？

A：I don't want to talk about it right now. It's a long story.
我現在不想談。事情說來話長。

相關用法

例 I don't want to talk about it.
我不想說。

例 Not now, please.
　拜託，現在別問！

例 It's certainly not easy for me, either
　對我來說也是不簡單的！

🎵 184

● 易如反掌

It's a piece of cake.

這太簡單了。

"a piece of cake" 字面意思是「一片蛋糕」，隱喻「事情太簡單了」，類似中文「易如反掌」的情境。

A：Would you show me how to do it?
　你能示範給我看如何作嗎？

B：Sure. It's piece of cake!
　當然好。這太簡單了！

類似用法

例 It's an easy cake.
　小事一樁。

例 No sweat.
　沒問題！

例 No problem.
　沒問題！

● 認錯

It's my fault.

這都是我的錯。

> 道歉的方法有很多種，除了"I am sorry"
> 之外，也可以用承認錯誤"my fault"來表示
> 認錯的歉意。

A：I was really wondering why it happened.

我實在懷疑這件事為什麼會發生。

B：It's my fault.

這都是我的錯。

同義用法

例 My mistake.
我的錯。

例 My fault.
我的錯。

例 My bad.
我的錯。

例 I made a mistake.
我做錯了。

> A：I made a mistake.
> 我做錯了。
> B：Why? What did you do?
> 為什麼這麼說？你做了什麼事？

MP3 186

●坦白説明

Let's get it straight.

我們開門見山吧！

希望彼此能夠開門見山地説明白，而不要有所隱藏時，就可以説"get it straight"，表示直來直往的率真態度。

A：Let's see. I think we should...

我想一想。我覺得我們應該…

B：Let's get it straight. What are you trying to say?

我們開門見山吧！你想要説什麼？

類似用法

例 Let's get it clear.
我們坦白地説吧！

例 Just tell me the truth.
只要告訴我事實！

相關用法

例 Let's put it this way.
這麼説吧！

MP3 187

●事情會雨過天晴

It's going to be over soon.

事情很快就會過去的。

"It's going to be over soon."是一種安慰的語句，希望對方能夠撐過這段難熬的日子。

A : I just can't stop thinking about it.

　　我就是無法不去想！

B : It's going to be over soon.

　　事情很快就會過去了。

類似用法

例 It will all work out.

　　事情會有辦法解決的。

例 Don't let the failure get you down.

　　不要讓這次的失敗使你沮喪。

例 The bad news got them down.

　　壞消息使他們很沮喪。

 188

● 臆測會發生

It's going to happen.

事情百分百確定了。

　　雖然不是鐵口直斷，但是你敢掛保證，
事情絕對會如同你所臆測般發展。

A : I don't think it's a good idea.

　　我覺得這不是一個好主意。

B : What can we say? It's going to happen.

　　我們還能說什麼？事情已經百分百確定
　　了。

類似用法

例 It's for sure.

　　確定了！

例 Definitely.
沒錯！

例 I can expect it.
我想也是！

例 I'm sure it is.
我認為的確是！

MP3 189

● 沒什麼大不了

It's no big deal.

沒什麼大不了！

> 看著對方緊張兮兮甚至不知所措時，你就可以老神在在地說："no big deal"表示你的鎮定態度。

A：Sorry, I couldn't make it.
抱歉，我無法過去。

B：Don't worry. It's no big deal.
別擔心！沒什麼大不了的！

同義用法

例 No big deal.
沒什麼大不了！

類似用法

例 Cut it out.
省省力氣吧！

●挑釁

So what?

那又怎樣？

> "So what?"具有非常挑釁的意味，意思就
> 是「事情就是如此，那又如何？」類似的說
> 法還有"So?"

A：How could you do this to me?

你怎麼可以如此對待我？

B：So what? I don't care at all.

那又怎樣？我一點都不在意。

相關用法

例 So?

那又如何？

例 What are you trying to say?

你想要說什麼？

●少管閒事

It's none of your business!

你少管閒事！

> 希望對方不要好管閒事，就可以說"none
> of your business"，或是希望對方管好自己
> 的事也可以說"mind your own business"。

A：You should save money for your coming baby boy.

你應該為你們即將出世的小男孩存錢。

B：It's none of your business!

你少管閒事！

同義用法

例 Mind your own business.

別多管閒事！

例 None of your business!

要你管？

例 This is totally not your business!

這裡沒你的事！

 192

● 重點

It's not the point.

這不是重點。

若是對方的所言已經偏離主題，你就可以適時點醒對方："It's not the point."表示「這不是事情的重點。」

A：Are you saying not to complete it?

你是說不要去完成嗎？

B：You are wrong. It's not the point.

你錯了。那不是重點。

類似用法

例 You missed the point.

這不是重點！

例 It's great, but it's not the point.

是很好，但這不是重點。

相關用法

例 What's the point?
重點是什麼？

例 To the point, please.
請說重點！

 193

● 發生什麼事
What happened?
發生了什麼事？

> 當發覺事有蹊蹺，千萬要記得問："What happened?"以瞭解事情的來龍去脈。

A : You look upset. What happened?
你看起來很憂愁。發生什麼事了？

B : We've just lost one of our best friends.
我們剛剛失去了一位好友。

類似用法

例 What's going on?
發生什麼事了？

例 What's wrong?
有什麼問題嗎？

例 What's the matter with you?
有什麼問題嗎？

MP3 194

● 懷疑有問題發生

What's the problem?

有什麼問題嗎？

> "What's the problem?"適用在探討事件發
> 生的問題癥結。若是問："What's your prob-
> lem?"則是質疑對方「腦袋有問題」！

A : You look terrible. What's the problem, Susan?

　　妳看起來糟透了。蘇珊，有什麼問題嗎？

B : I don't feel well.

　　我覺得不舒服。

類似用法

例 Something happened.
不太對勁喔！

例 There must be something.
事情不太對！

例 Is there something wrong?
有問題嗎？

例 Is that a problem?
有問題嗎？

MP3 195

● 詢問有沒有問題

Any problem?

有沒有問題？

> 想要知道對方還有沒有其他問題要問時，
> 可以用"Any problem?"來探詢對方的想法。

A : Any problem?

　　有沒有問題？

B : No. Thanks for asking.

　　沒有！謝謝關心！

類似用法

例 Any questions?

　　有任何問題嗎？

例 Do you have any questions?

　　還有問題嗎？

 196

● 詢問有什麼事要說
What's up?

什麼事？

"What's up?" 除了是關心對方的近況之外，對方有話要說卻「欲言又止」時，可以是你的關心問句，或是當事情發生時，你的第一個反射性問題。

A : Hey, David, got a minute?

　　嘿，大衛，有空嗎？

B : Sure. What's up?

　　當然。有事嗎？

類似用法

例 Yes?

　　怎麼啦？

例 What's wrong?

怎麼啦？

MP3 197

● 深感遺憾

I'm sorry to hear that.

真是遺憾！

當聽到不好的消息時，你深表遺憾及同情，就可以說："Sorry to hear that."以表達你的感同身受。

A：My father has been sick for three weeks.

我父親已經病了三星期。

B：I'm sorry to hear that.

真是遺憾！

MP3 198

● 表達歉意

I'm sorry.

抱歉。

表達歉意最直接、最實用的語句就是"I'm sorry."

A：I'm sorry.

抱歉。

B：It doesn't matter.

不要緊的！

例 Sorry for that.
我為此事感到抱歉！

例 Sorry.
抱歉！

> A：Sorry.
>   抱歉！
> B：For what?
>   為什麼要道歉？

例 I'm sorry about the whole thing.
這整件事我感到很抱歉。

相關用法

例 I'm sorry for what I have said to you.
我為我向你說過的話表示道歉。

例 Sorry. I didn't mean to hurt your feelings.
對不起！我沒有傷害你的意思。

例 Sorry for causing so much trouble.
抱歉引起這麼多麻煩！

例 I must apologize for not answering your call in time.
我必須為沒有及時回電給你而道歉。

例 I'm afraid I've brought you too much trouble.
我想我已經給你帶來了太多的麻煩。

●請求原諒

Forgive me.

原諒我！

雖沒有直接說出「道歉」，但是"forgive me"已經有「認錯」、「請求原諒」的意思了。

A：Would you forgive me?

你願意原諒我嗎？

B：I already did.

我已經原諒你了！

類似用法

例 God, please forgive me.
上帝啊！請原諒我。

例 Please forgive my mistake.
請原諒我的過錯！

例 Sorry, I didn't mean that.
抱歉，我不是有意的！

相關用法

例 I will forgive you.
我會原諒你！

●回應原諒與遺憾
That's all right.

沒關係！

> 當對方向你道歉，你就必須有雅量去原諒對方的錯誤："That's all right."並接受道歉"I accept your apology."

A：Excuse me for being late.

對不起，我遲到了。

B：That's all right.

沒關係！

類似用法

例 That's OK.

沒關係！

例 Never mind.

不要在意！

例 Please don't worry about that.

請別為此事擔心！

●同感高興
I'm glad to hear that.

我很高興知道這件事。

> 替對方感到高興的欣慰語句："so glad to hear that"以表示你為對方感到高興。

A：I'm going to study in L.A.

我就要去洛杉磯唸書了。

B：I'm glad to hear that. When are you leaving for L.A.?

我很高興知道這件事。你什麼時候要啟程去洛杉磯？

同義用法

例 I'm happy to hear that.

我很高興聽見這件事。

類似用法

例 I'm really happy for you.

我真為你感到高興。

例 Good for you.

對你來說是好事。

MP3 202

● 惋惜

That's too bad.

太可惜了！

當壞事發生在親友身上時，你的安慰與不捨絕對是必要的："That's too bad."

A：I didn't get that job.

我沒有得到那份工作。

B：How come? That's too bad. You are the best in this field.

為什麼？太可惜了！你是這個領域中的箇中好手。

同義用法

例 Too bad.
太可惜了！

例 I'm sorry to hear that.
我很遺憾聽見這件事。

類似用法

例 No way.
不會吧！

 203

● 事情很難熬

It's so hard for you.

這對你來説真是困難。

> 當親友面臨人生莫大的考驗時，拍拍對方的肩膀説聲："It's so hard for you."表示難為對方了，順便安慰對方："Don't worry. You have us."（別擔心，你有我們陪你！）

A：Don't worry. It will all work out.

別擔心，事情總會有辦法解決的。

B：It's so hard for you.

這對你來説真是困難。

同義用法

例 It's not easy for you.
難為你了！

例 It must be tough.
真是難為你了！

例 It's not an easy job.
真是一項不簡單的工作！

相關用法

例 It's not easy being a parent.
父母難為！

🎵 204

● 不認同

That's what you say.

那只是你個人的看法。

> 認為這只是對方單方面的想法時，就可
> 以說：**"That's what you say."**表示「我不認
> 同你的言論。」

A：I think Mr. Jones does not agree with you
on this point.

我覺得瓊斯先生就這件事和你的看法不
同。

B：That's what you say.

那只是你個人的看法。

相關用法

例 I don't think so.
我不這麼認為！

例 Bad idea.
這主意不好！

例 It won't work.
這行不通的！

例 I'm afraid not.

恐怕不可以！

MP3 205

● 檢視自己
Look at you.

看看你！

表示對方的模樣應該是很困窘、甚至是不堪，所以要對方好好反省檢討一番。

A：Look at you. What happened to you?

看看你！你怎麼了？

B：I was punched by my brother.

我被我兄弟打。

A：Poor baby.

可憐的傢伙！

MP3 206

● 對方看起來糟透了
You look terrible.

你看起來糟透了！

當你看見對方的狀況簡直慘不忍睹時，問問對方："You look terrible." 還要記得不吝嗇付出你的關心："Are you OK?"

A：You look terrible. What happened to you?

你看起來糟透了！你怎麼了？

B：I broke my leg last night.

我昨晚摔斷腿了！

類似用法

例 You look like shit.

你看起來簡直可怕極了！

MP3 207

●期待

I look forward to it.

我很期待這件事。

"look forward to + 某事"是常用片語，表示「期待某事發生」的意思，例如"I look forward to this game."（我很期待這場比賽。）

A：Are you going to David's birthday party?

你有要去參加大衛的生日派對嗎？

B：Of course. I look forward to it.

當然！我很期待這件事。

A：Great. Can I go with you?

太好了！我可以和你一起去嗎？

同義用法

例 I'm looking forward to it.

我很期待這件事！

例 I'm looking forward to this party.

我很期待這次的派對。

相關用法

例 I'm looking forward to seeing you.

我很期待與你見面。

例 We're looking forward to your visit.
我們相當期待你的來訪！

● 有道理
It made sense.
有道理！

> "make sense"是常用片語，表示「事情是合理的」，例如當你認同對方的看法時，並覺得有道理時，就可以說："It made sense."

A：Don't you think we should go there by train? It's already ten-thirty now.
　　你不覺得我們應該要搭火車去嗎？現在已經十點卅分了！

B：It made sense.
　　有道理！

同義用法

例 That made sense.
那是有道理的。

例 That made perfect sense.
真是太有道理了！

反義用法

例 It made no sense.
莫名其妙。

例 It's nonsense.
沒道理！

MP3 209

●別急

Take your time.

慢慢來不要急。

> 台語有一句諺語：「吃緊弄破碗」，表示
> 欲速則不達的意思，所以當你看見某人匆
> 匆忙忙時，你就可以安撫對方："Take your
> time."表示「不要急、慢慢來」。

A：Out of my way. It's too late now.
　　滾開，現在太晚了！

B：Take your time.
　　慢慢來，不要急！

類似用法

例 It's not urgent.
事情沒有那麼緊急。

例 Relax!
放輕鬆！

相關用法

例 Take a deep breath.
深呼吸一下！

MP3 210

● 勸人慢慢來

Slow down.

慢慢說！

"slow down"是常用片語，是告訴匆匆忙忙的人，「慢一點、別急」的意思，不論說話、行動的情境都適用。

A：David, did you know...

大衛，你知道嗎…？

B：Hey, slow down. What's going on?

嘿，慢慢說！怎麼啦？

MP3 211

● 動腦筋

Use your head.

用用你的腦袋吧！

當對方完全不動腦筋，只希望答案從天上掉下來不勞而獲時，你就可以告訴對方："Use your head."表示「你自己動動腦筋吧！」另一種意思則是要對方自行思考、判斷！

A：I have no idea what is going on here.

我不知道這裡發生了什麼事。

B：Use your head, idiot.

用用你的腦袋吧，笨蛋！

類似用法

例 You do the math.
你自己算!

例 Say something.
説説話吧!

例 What's your opinion?
你的想法呢?

MP3 212

●目前不確定

We will see.

再説吧!

> 當有人提出要求,而你還不願意正面回應他 yes 或 no 時,就可以先擱置著不回答,只要告訴對方:"We will see."表示「再説吧!我還沒決定!」

A : Mom, can I go to Jack's home and stay the night?

媽,我可以去傑克家過夜嗎?

B : We will see.

再説吧!

A : Please!

拜託啦!

相關用法

例 It's not a good time to talk about it.
現在不是談論的好時機!

例 Maybe.

也許是！

MP3 213

● 互相幫忙
What are friends for?

朋友就是要互相幫助！

> 中文有一句話叫做「兩肋插刀」，英文中
> 也有類似的情境，表示你願意為朋友付出："
> **What are friends for?**"表示「朋友是做什麼
> 用的？就是要互相幫忙啊！」

A：I don't know how to thank you.

我真不知道該如何感謝你。

B：Oh, come on. What are friends for?

喔！拜託。朋友就是要互相幫助！

MP3 214

● 共度難關
You have us.

你有我們（陪你）啊！

> 當朋友處在人生的低潮或遇到難關時，
> 身為朋友的你，的確有義務伸出援手！

A：I really don't know what to do.

我真的不知道該怎麼辦！

B：Don't worry about it. You have us.

別擔心！你有我們(陪你)啊！

類似用法

例 I'll be here with you.
我會陪你度過一切！

相關用法

例 I know how you feel.
我瞭解你的感受！

🎵 215

● 趕路

What's the hurry?

趕什麼？

> 當你看到對方似乎匆匆忙忙行走的時候，就可以問問對方："What's the hurry?"表示「你要趕著去哪裡，怎麼這麼匆忙？」

A：Hey, kids, what's the hurry?
　　嗨，孩子們，你們在趕什麼？

B：We have to catch the school bus.
　　我們要去趕搭校車。

同義用法

例 What's the rush!
急什麼！

例 Why are you hurrying?
你為什麼這麼趕？

● 離開

I have to go.

我要走了。

> "I have to go."是要說道別前的提示,表示快要離開了、準備要道別了,若有話還沒有說完的,請趕快說!

A:Can't you stay for dinner?

你不能留下來吃晚餐嗎?

B:Sorry. I really have to go.

抱歉,我真的要走了。

同義用法

例 I've got to go.
我必須要走了。

例 I'll be leaving.
我要離開了。

例 It's about time to say good-bye.
該是說再見的時候了。

例 Time to say good-bye now.
現在該是說再見的時候了!

相關用法

例 Are you taking off?
你要走了嗎?

MP3 217

● 要去哪裡

Where are you off to?

你(們)要去哪裡？

在路上遇到認識的人，就可以隨口問一句：**"Where are you off to?"** 表示「你要去哪裡啊？」

A：Where are you guys off to?

你們一群人要去哪裡？

B：We are going to see a movie.

我們要去看電影。

同義用法

例 Where are you going?
你要去哪裡？

例 Where are you headed?
你要去哪裡？

MP3 218

● 說話被中斷

Where was I?

（剛剛）我說到哪？

若是說話被中斷，要再回復到先前話題時，有可能一下子記不起來剛剛說到哪，就可以說：**"Where was I?"**，這裡可不是問「我人在哪裡」的意思，別誤會囉！

A：So we have to...

所以我們必須要…

B：Say no more.

別再説了！

C：Excuse me, where is the post office?

抱歉，請問郵局在哪裡？

A：Post office? Turn right and you will see it.

郵局？右轉你就會看到。

C：Thanks.

謝謝你！

A：Sure. Uh... where was I?

不必客氣！嗯…(剛剛)我説到哪？

MP3 219

●不用提醒

You are telling me.

還用得著你説！

當你已經知道某種結果時，對方卻又自
以為聰明地提示你或下結論，你就可以有
點調侃、不耐地説："You are telling me."表
示「我已經知道了，還用得著你多嘴！」

A：You are fired.

你被炒魷魚了。

B：You are telling me.

不必你多説，我已經知道了。

220

●請對方提出建議

You tell me.

你說呢？

> "You tell me."的字面意思雖然是指「你告訴我」，但其實是指「希望能得到你的建議或意見」。

A：How can you solve this problem by your-self?

你怎麼能自己解決這個問題呢？

B：You tell me.

你說呢？

類似用法

例 What's your opinion?

你的意見呢？

例 What will you advise?

你的建議呢？

例 I need your advice.

我需要你的建議！

 221

●舉出實例

Such as?

例如什麼？

> 當對方提出建議後，你覺得還需要具體的例子才能理解，就可以說"Such as? "表示你還不是很明白，請對方再說清楚些，最好還能舉出例子。

A：Maybe we should give her a surprise.

也許我們可以給她一個驚喜！

B：Such as?

例如什麼？

A：I have no idea.

我不知道耶！

同義用法

例 For example?

例如什麼？

A：We need to do something special.

我們需要做一點特別的事！

B：For example?

例如什麼？

A：A birthday party?

生日派對如何？

 222

● 提出保證

You have my word.

我向你保證。

「我向你保證」是一種承諾，表示「言出必行」，可以用："You have my word."表示，"word"是表示承諾。另一種常見的說法則是："I promise."

A：How can I trust you? You promise?

我如何能相信你？你保證？

B：You have my word.
我向你保證。

類似用法

📗 I give you my word for it.
我向你保證。

📗 Take my word for it.
我向你保證。

📗 I promise you.
我向你保證。

📗 I promise.
我保證。

相關用法

📗 He promised it to me.
他有向我保證過！

📗 You promised.
你答應過我的。

 223

● 準備妥當
Are you ready?

準備好了嗎？

> 「準備」叫做"be ready"，通常是表示一切就緒，準備要做某事的意思。

A：Are you ready?
準備好了嗎？

B：Ready for what?

　　準備好什麼？

A：Our wedding! My God. You totally forgot it?

　　我們的婚禮啊！我的老天爺啊！你完全忘記了？

MP3 224

● 受驚嚇

You scared me!

你嚇到我了。

> 表示自己被對方突如其來的動作或言論驚嚇，就可以說："You scared me!" 表示「你害我嚇一跳！」

A：Hey, pal, what are you doing here?

　　嘿，兄弟，你在這裡幹嘛？

B：My God! You scared me!

　　我的天啊！你嚇到我了。

類似用法

例 What a shock.
　 真是訝異！

例 Holy shit.
　 天啊！

例 Oh, my.
　 喔！我的天啊！

MP3 225

● 抱怨

It sucks.

糟透了！

"suck"一般的認知是「吸吮」的意思，但有另一種俚語的用法，表示「很爛」、「很糟糕」的意思。例如朋友問你某個餐廳的食物好不好吃，你就可以說："That sucks."表示「難吃斃了」！

A：What do you think of this movie?

你覺得這部電影如何？

B：It sucks.

糟透了！

類似用法

例 That sucks.

很爛！

例 This show sucks.

這場秀很爛！

例 This place sucks.

這個地方真是爛透了！

A：Hey, honey, are you OK?

嘿，親愛的，你還好吧？

B：Can't we go somewhere else? This place sucks.

我們不能去其他地方嗎？這個地方真是爛透了！

● 對方將會遺憾
You'll be sorry.

你會後悔的！

表示對方如果不聽勸告，將來一定會後悔，就用未來式表示："You'll be sorry."這可不是「你將來會道歉」，其中的"sorry"是指「遺憾」、「後悔」的意思。

A：I still want to go out with Kenny.

我還是希望和肯尼出去。

B：You will be sorry.

你會後悔的！

類似用法

（例）You'll be sorry for that.

你會為那件事後悔的。

（例）I believe you will regret doing this.

我相信你會為這麼做而後悔的。

相關用法

（例）I'm regretful about it.

我很遺憾！

（例）I'm so sorry.

我很遺憾！

227

●央求

Please?

拜託啦！

中文的「拜託」在英文中並沒有相對應的翻譯說法，可以直接用"please"（請）這個字表示。

A：Can I go swimming with Kenny?

我可以和肯尼去游泳嗎？

B：I don't think so.

不可以！

A：Please?

拜託啦！

 228

●答應

Go ahead.

隨你便。

答應對方的要求除了簡單地說"yes"之外，也可以說："Go ahead."特別適用在對方詢問是否可以做某事或去某地時的情境問句的回答。"Go ahead."還有另一種意思，表示「隨便你，我不管你」的意思。

A：I quit. I can't finish it by myself.

我放棄。我無法自己一個人完成。

B：Fine. Go ahead.

好啊！隨你便。

同義用法

例 Sure.

　好啊！

例 No problem.

　沒問題！

反義用法

例 No way.

　不可以！

例 No, I don't think so.

　不，我不這麼認為！

例 No, you can't do it.

　不行，你不可以這麼做！

例 I don't think so.

　你想都別想！

> A：Maybe we can go swimming?
>
> 　也許我們可以去游泳？
>
> B：I don't think so.
>
> 　你想都別想！

MP3 229

● 沒意見

That's fine by me.

我沒意見。

> 表示你所提出的提議、看法…等，「我都沒有意見」，等於是答應的意思。

A : What would you like for breakfast? How about a sandwich?

早餐你想吃什麼？要不要三明治？

B : That's fine by me.

我沒意見。

同義用法

例 Fine.

好啊！

例 Sure.

好啊！

例 No problem.

沒問題！

例 Why not.

有何不可！

MP3 230

● 否決

Absolutely not.

絕對不可以。

"Absolutely not."特別強調「絕對不可以」的意思。

A : Mom, can I go camping with Kenny?

媽，我可以和肯尼去露營嗎？

B : Absolutely not.

絕對不可以！

例 No way.
想都別想！

例 Of course not.
當然不可以。

例 I'd rather you didn't.
最好不要！

例 Not on your life.
一輩子都別想！

例 Go ahead.
可以！

 231

● 輕微的情況
Kind of.

有一點。

當對方猜測你的狀況時，你可以說"Kind of."，表示「情況是有一點如你所說」。非常適用在個人現在所處的情況中。

A：Are you still upset?
你還在難過嗎？

B：Kind of.
還有一點（難過）。

A：Don't worry about it. She will make a good wife.

不要擔心！她會是一個好妻子的。

類似用法

例 Sort of.
有一點！

例 A little bit.
有一點！

相關用法

例 Yes and no.
也是也不是！

> A：You will call her, won't you?
> 你會打電話給她，對嗎？
> B：Yes and no.
> 也是也不是。

 232

● 循規蹈矩

Behave yourself !

你守規矩點！

"Behave yourself !"字面意思是指「要表現得像你自己」，也就是警告、規勸對方不要不守規矩時使用。

A：Mom, Jack is trying to punch me again.

媽，傑克又要打我了。

B：Jack, behave yourself.

傑克，你守規矩點！

例 You had better behave.

你最好行為檢點些。

例 Be your age.

別孩子氣了！

例 Grow up.

成熟點吧！

例 You're a big girl now.

妳已經長大了！

（對方為女性）

例 You're a big boy now.

你已經長大了！

（對方為男性）

MP3 233

● 結帳

Bill, please.

請買單。

千萬別把"Bill"當成人名的「比爾」，這裡的"Bill, please."指的是「請拿帳單給我結帳」的意思。

A：Server! Bill, please.

侍者，請結帳。

B：Would you please wait for a moment?

請稍等好嗎？

A：No problem.

沒問題！

類似用法

例 Check, please.

請買單。

例 I want my bill, please.

我要結帳。

例 May I have the bill, please?

請給我帳單好嗎？

MP3 234

●叫救護車

Call an ambulance.

打電話叫救護車！

發生意外時，請記得要"Call an ambulance."表示「打電話叫救護車！」

A：Do you want me to call an ambulance?

需要我打電話叫救護車嗎？

B：Yes, please do it for me.

好的，請為我這麼做。

A：I'll be right back with you. Hang on.

我馬上回來。撐著點！

類似用法

例 Call me an ambulance.
幫我打電話叫救護車!

例 We need to call an ambulance right now.
我們現在要立刻叫救護車。

相關用法

例 Could you send me a doctor?
能為我請個醫生來嗎?

 235

● 稱讚

Wonderful!

太棒了!

> 對方的表現實在值得你讚美時,就說:
> "Wonderful!"或是"Well done."表示「太棒
> 了!」

A : I have to stop smoking.

　　我必需要戒煙。

B : Wonderful! That's good for you.

　　太好了。那對你很好。

類似用法

例 Great.
很好!

例 Good.
不錯喔!

例 Brilliant.

太好了！

例 Terrific.

太好了！

MP3 236

● 稱讚優良表現

Good job.

幹得好！

和前一句一樣都是讚美，但是是針對「良好的工作表現」時，就可以說：**"Good job."** 表示中文「幹得好！」的意思。

A：I've already finished it on time.

我已經如期完成了。

B：Good job.

很好。

A：You really think so?

你真這麼認為嗎？

類似用法

例 Nice work.

幹得好！

例 Well done.

幹得好！

例 Nice going.

幹得好！

例 Very good.
很好。

例 You did a great job.
你做得很好。

● 稱讚對方很炫

Cool!

真酷！

"Cool!"是常見於年輕人之間的用法，表示令人羨慕、很炫、很酷的意思。

A：Look! This is a brand new robot!

看！這是一部全新的機器人。

B：Cool. Where did you get this?

好酷喔！哪來的？

A：It's a birthday present.

是生日禮物！

類似用法

例 It's so cool!
真酷！

例 It's awesome.
真酷！

例 That's really something.
真是了不起！

MP3 238

● 感恩的稱讚

It's very kind of you.

你真是個好人。

> 表示對方非常好心、善解人意、幫了大忙…等，都可以說："It's very kind of you." 表示「你真是個大好人啊！」

A：Look out! It's pretty dangerous.

　　小心，很危險的。

B：Thank you. It's very kind of you.

　　謝謝你，你真是個好人。

A：Don't mention it.

　　不必客氣！

類似用法

例 It's very kind of you, David.
　 大衛，你真是好心。

例 You are so nice.
　 你真是好心。

例 That's nice of you.
　 你真好！

相關用法

例 You're a very kind and thoughtful person.
　 你真是好心又細心的人。

●探詢是否有人

Hello?

有人嗎？

"Hello?"雖是打招呼的「哈囉」，也適用在詢問「這裡有人嗎」的情境，若是有人在這裡，對方就會說："Over here."表示「我人在這裡。」

A：Hello? Anybody here?

哈囉，有人嗎？

B：May I help you?

需要我幫忙嗎？

A：Yes. Can you call me an ambulance? I feel sick.

是的。可以幫我叫一部救護車嗎？我覺得不舒服。

類似用法

例 Anybody here?

有人嗎？

例 Anybody home?

有人在家嗎？

MP3 240

●求救

Help.

救命啊！

遇到緊急事件需要外界的幫助時，請大聲呼喊："Help!"這就是中文的「救命啊！」的意思。

A：Help. Help.

救命啊！救命啊！

B：What's wrong, madam?

小姐，怎麼啦？

MP3 241

●請對方等候

Hold on.

等一下。

不論任何原因，請對方「稍候」，就可以說"Hold on."或是"Hold on a second"。 再加"a second"是表示「很短暫的時間」。

A：May I speak to Mr. Wilkins?

請問威爾金斯先生在嗎？

B：Hold on, please. I will get him.

請等一下，我去找他來接電話。

同義用法

例 Hold on a second.

等一下。

例 Just a minute, please.
請等一下。

例 One moment, please.
請等一下。

例 Wait a moment.
等一下。

MP3 242

●不要來騷擾
Stay away from me!
離我遠一點！

希望對方不要像蒼蠅一樣整天繞著你轉，記請對方「待在遠一點的地方」，英文就叫做"stay away"，若是要特別強調「少靠近我」，就說"Stay away from me!"意思就是叫對方「滾遠一點」！

A：What are you doing here, Susan?
蘇珊，妳在這裡做什麼？

B：Stay away from me!
離我遠一點！

類似用法

例 Leave me alone.
別管我！

例 Go fly a kite and stop bugging me.
走開，別煩我！

例 Get lost.
滾蛋！

MP3 243

●面對現實

Face it.

面對現實吧！

有人成天做白日夢，當個縮頭烏龜、不願面對現實時，你可以告誡他："Face it."表示「勇敢些，面對現實吧！」

A : I don't know why she always turns me down.

我不知道她為什麼老是拒絕我。

B : Face it. She doesn't like you at all.

面對現實吧！她一點都不喜歡你。

類似用法

例 Let's face this problem.
讓我們面對這個難關吧！

相關用法

例 It's the real world.
這是個現實的社會！

MP3 244

●放棄

I quit!

我不幹了！

表示你不願意再繼續進行某一件事時，就可以說"I quit!"表示你放棄了、不願意再這麼做的意思。

A : You know what? I quit!

你知道嗎？我不幹了！

B : Come on, man. I can't do that without you.

老兄，不要這樣！沒有你我實在辦不到。

MP3 245

●請求指引方向
Could you tell me the way to the post office?

要怎麼到郵局去？

> 請求「指引方向」就叫做"tell me the way"，所以要問「要如何到某地去？」就叫做"could you tell me the way to +地點?"

A : Excuse me, could you tell me the way to the post office?

請問一下，要怎麼到郵局去？

B : Turn right at the second crossing.

在第二個十字路口向右轉。

類似用法

⑩ How can I get to the post office?

要如何到郵局呢？

⑩ Excuse me, but where is the post office?

請問一下，郵局在哪兒？

例 Could you show me the way to the post office?

你能指去郵局的路嗎？

例 Could you tell me how I can get to the post office?

你能告訴我怎樣到郵局嗎？

MP3 246

● 詢問道路所到的目的

Is this the road to the post office?

這是去郵局的路嗎？

若要確定這條路的盡頭或所經過的路線，可以問："Is this the road to + 地點?" 表示「這是去某地的路嗎？」

A：Excuse me, is this the road to the post office?

請問一下，這是去郵局的路嗎？

B：That's right.

沒錯！

同義用法

例 Does this street lead to the post office?

這條街通往郵局嗎？

●請求指引所在的位置

Where am I on the map?

我在地圖上的哪裡？

> 當你手上有地圖卻又迷路時，最好的方法就是請求對方告訴你「我現在在地圖上的哪個地點上」："Where am I on the map?" 表示「我在地圖上的哪裡？」

A：Where am I on the map?

我在地圖上的哪裡？

B：Sure. Let me see your map.

好的！給我看你的地圖。

類似用法

例 Would you mind drawing me a map on this piece of paper?

請你在這張紙上給我畫個路線圖好嗎？

●迷路了

I think I'm lost here.

我想我可能迷路了。

> 「迷路」就表示「迷失方向」的意思，所以可以用"lost"來表示，若是要說「我迷路了」就可以說："I'm lost."

A：May I help you?

需要我幫忙嗎？

B：Yes. I think I'm lost here.

是的！我想我可能迷路了。

類似用法

例 I don't know where I am now.

我不知道我現在在哪裡。

 249

● 陪同至目的地

I'll walk you there.

我陪你走過去。

利用一小段時間陪同對方走到某地，可以用"walk"這個動詞，且多半使用未來式句型，所以「我陪你走過去」是"I will walk you there."

A：Excuse me, sir, but could you please tell me how to get to the post office?

對不起，先生，請問到郵局怎麼走？

B：I'll walk you there. It's on my route.

我陪你走過去。我正好路過那兒。

 250

● 步行所花的時間

It's about 10 minutes' walk.

步行大約需要十分鐘。

「步行時間」叫做"分鐘+ walk"，舉例來說，若是「廿分鐘的步行時間」就叫做"20 minutes' walk"，記住，"minute"（分鐘）的複數所格式是用"minutes' "來表示。

A：Oh, such a long way!

　　噢，好遠啊！

B：That's right. It's about 10 minutes' walk.

　　沒錯！步行大約需要十分鐘。

類似用法

例 It's about 10 minutes' ride from here.

　　從這兒大約十分鐘車程。

相關用法

例 Well, it's a long way from here.

　　噢，那裡離這兒很遠耶！

MP3 251

●指引搭公車
You can take bus No. 15.

可以搭 15 號公車。

「公車車號」是以"bus + No. 號碼"表示即可，"No."是"Number"的縮寫。而「搭乘公車」所使用的動詞是"take"。

A：Well, it's a long way from here.

　　噢，那裡離這兒很遠耶！

B：Yes, but you can take bus No. 15. It will take you right there.

　　是啊，不過你可以搭 15 號公車。它會載你到那裏。

相關用法

例 The bus stop is just over there.

公共汽車站就在那邊。

MP3 252

● 自己也不認得路

I'm a stranger here, too.

我也是第一次來這兒。

> 若是有人向你問路,而你對這個地方也
> 不熟悉,就等於你「在當地也算是個陌生
> 人」,英文就可以說:"I'm a stranger here,
> too."表示「我也是第一次來這附近,所以
> 我不熟悉路況」。

A:Could you please tell me how I can arrive
at the Taipei Station?

請問到台北車站怎麼走?

B:Oh, I'm very sorry, but I'm a stranger here,
too.

非常抱歉,我也是第一次來這兒。

MP3 253

● 去電找人

May I speak to David?

請找大衛接電話好嗎?

> 告訴接電話者「要找某一位受話方來接
> 電話」,直接使用"speak"這個動詞即可,
> 就叫做"May I speak to + 名字?"

A：Hello. May I speak to David?

你好！請找大衛接電話好嗎？

B：Hold the line, please.

請稍等。

同義用法

例 Is David there?

大衛在嗎？

例 I want to speak to David.

我想和大衛通話。

 254

●受話方是否在
Is David around?

大衛在嗎？

直接詢問接電話的人「某人是否在」就可以問："Is David around?"，字面意思類似「某人是否在那裡」。

A：Is David around?

大衛在嗎？

B：Who is speaking, please?

請問你是哪一位？

類似用法

例 Is David in, please?

請問大衛在嗎？

例 Is David in the office?

大衛有在辦公室裡嗎？

MP3 255

●本人接電話

This is he.

我就是本人。

若是來電者要找的本人接的電話,接電話者若是男性,就可以直接說:"This is he."而女性則是"This is she."記住,不可以說"I am",也不能將 he 或 she 改成 him 或 her。

A：May I speak to David, please?

請問大衛在嗎?

B：This is he.

我就是。

A：Hi, David, this is Tom.

嗨,大衛,我是湯姆!

同義用法

例 Speaking.

我就是。

> A：Is Mr. Brown in?
> 布朗先生在嗎?
> B：Speaking.
> 我就是。

類似用法

例 This is David speaking.

我是大衛。

相關用法

例 This is she.

我就是本人！

（說話者為女性）

🎵 256

● 代為記下留言

May I take a message?

需要我幫你留言嗎？

接電話者要幫來電者「記下留言」，一定是使用"take a message"這個慣用語，因此詢問「需要我幫你留言嗎？」就可以說"May I take a message?"

A：May I take a message?

需要我幫你留言嗎？

B：Sure. Please tell her David called.

好的！請告訴她大衛有來電。

類似用法

例 Would you like to leave a message?

需要留言嗎？

相關用法

例 What is it, please?

請問留什麼話？

> A：I am her friend. May I leave a message?
>
> 　　我是她朋友。我可以留言嗎？
>
> B：Just a moment, please. I need to get a pencil.
>
> 　　OK. What is it, please?
>
> 　　請稍等。我需要支鉛筆。好啦，請問留
> 　　什麼話？

MP3 257

●詢問對方的電話號碼

What's your number, please?

請問你的號碼是多少？

> 「電話號碼」是"telephone number"，但
> 是美國人通常都直接說"number"，因此要
> 問對方的電話號碼是多少，就可以直接說：
> "What's your number?"

A：What's your number, please?

　　請問你的號碼是多少？

B：86473663. My extension is 274.

　　86473663。我的分機是274。

 258

●要求留言

May I leave a message?

我可以留言嗎？

> "May I leave a message?"是詢問「能否
> 留言」的萬用語句。記住，「留下留言」一
> 定要使用"leave"這個動詞。

A：May I leave a message?

我可以留言嗎？

B：Sure. Please let me get a pen.

好的！請先讓我拿支筆。

 259

●來電者請求代為轉告
Would you please tell her to call me back?

能請你告訴她回我電話好嗎？

> 「請求」的要求語句一定是"Would you please..."，而中文的「轉告某人」是沒有相對應的英文翻譯，只要用「告訴某人」："tell + 某人"的用法即可，所以「請求代為轉告回電」就可以說："Would you please tell him/her to call me back?"

A：May I take a message?

需要我幫你留言嗎？

B：Sure. Would you please tell her to call me back this afternoon? I'll be expecting her call then.

好的！能請你告訴她今天下午回個電話給我好嗎？我會等她電話。

MP3 260

● 詢問有沒有留言

Are there any messages for me?

有我的留言嗎？

"message"就是「留言」的意思，不管是電話留言、訪客留言…等都適用，若要問「有沒有給我的留言？」就可以說："Are there any messages for me?"

A：Are there any messages for me?

有我的留言嗎？

B：Yes, Mr. Smith. Your wife called this morning.

有的，史密斯先生，您的夫人今早有來電。

MP3 261

● 電話佔線中

The line is busy.

電話佔線中。

「電話佔線」怎麼說？只要用「線路很忙」的思考邏輯，就知道可以用"The line is busy"的表達方式。

A：Hello, is Susan in?

喂，蘇珊在嗎？

B：The line is busy. Would you like to leave a message?

電話佔線中。你要留言嗎？

類似用法

例 The line is engaged.
電話占線中。

MP3 262

● 電話中請對方稍等
Just a minute, please.

請稍等！

> 電話中請對方「稍候」可以使用的語句非常多，最常見的就是"Just a minute, ple-ase."或是直接說"Hold on."

A：Hello, may I speak to Susan, please?

喂，請讓蘇珊聽電話。

B：Oh, just a minute, please. Susan, it's for you.

哦，請稍等……。蘇珊，找妳的電話。

同義用法

例 Hold the line, please.
請稍等。

例 Hold on a second, please.
請稍等！

MP3 263

● 打錯電話

You must have dialed the wrong number.

你可能打錯電話了。

「撥打電話號碼」叫做"dial the number"
所以若是接到一通撥錯電話的來電，就可
以告訴對方"dial the wrong number"「你可
能打錯電話了。」

A：May I speak to Mr. Smith?

請問史密斯先生在嗎？

B：You must have dialed the wrong number.

你可能打錯電話了。

A：Sorry.

抱歉！

類似用法

 What is the number you are calling?

你打幾號？

MP3 264

● 詢問來電者身分

Who is it, please?

請問是哪位？

和詢問門外敲門者是誰一樣，詢問來電
者身分也是用"Who is it?"通常為了禮貌，
會再加「請問」，所以可以說："Who is it,
please?"

A：Hello, this is Jenny speaking. Who is it, please?

喂，我是珍妮，請問是哪位？

B：This is David speaking.

我是大衛。

同義用法

例 Who is speaking, please?

請問你是哪一位？

 265

● 趕搭交通工具

I have to catch a plane.

我要趕飛機。

> 不論要趕搭飛機、趕搭火車、趕搭公車，都可以用"catch"這個動詞。

A：What's the rush?

你趕著要去哪裡？

B：I have to catch a plane.

我要去趕飛機！

A：I can give you a lift.

我可以送你去！

相關用法

例 I don't know whether we can catch the train.

我不知道能否趕得上火車。

MP3 266

●航班查詢

Could you check the boarding time for me?

您能替我查班機時刻表嗎？

> 當你需要知道航班的抵達或離境時間，這是一句必備的問句："Could you check the boarding time?"

A：Could you check the boarding time for me?

能替我查班機時刻表嗎？

B：Which flight would you like to know?

您想要知道哪一個班次？

MP3 267

●詢問票價

How much is the airfare?

票價多少錢？

> "How much"是非常實用的句型，舉凡和價格相關的「多少錢」都適用。

A：How much is the airfare?

票價是多少錢？

B：It's two thousand dollars.

兩千元。

類似用法

例 I'd like to know the airfare.
我想要知道票價。

相關用法

例 What's the one-way fare?
單程票價是多少錢？

例 What's the fare from Taipei to Tokyo?
從台北到東京票價是多少錢？

 268

● 特定地點的機票預定

I want to make a reservation
from Taipei to New York.
我要預約從台北到紐約的機位。

"make a reservation"表示「預約」、「預定」的意思，不論是機位、餐廳訂位、約定會面等都適用。

A：Good morning. This is Chinese Airlines.
早安。這是中華航空。

B：I want to make a reservation from Taipei
to New York.
我要預約從台北到紐約的機位。

類似用法

例 I'd like to book two seats from Taipei to New York on August 25th.

我要訂兩個人在八月廿五日從台北到紐約的機位。

 269

● 特定日期的機票預定

I'd like to book the first flight to New York for May 1st.

我想預訂五月一日到紐約的最早航班。

"book"當成名詞是「書籍」，但若是動詞時，則表示是「預訂」的意思。應用在訂班機的情境時，最常用的片語為"book a flight"。

A：I'd like to book the first flight to New York for May 1st.

我想預訂五月一日到紐約的最早航班。

B：OK, sir.

好的，先生。

相關用法

例 Do you fly to New York on September 2nd?

你們有九月二日到紐約的班機嗎？

例 Do you fly from Taipei to New York on September 2nd?
你們有九月二日從台北到紐約的班機嗎？

例 I prefer a morning flight.
我偏好早上的班機。

🎵 270

● 訂直達航班
I'd like to book a nonstop flight.
我要訂直達的班機。

> 航班有分直達或轉機的不同，直達班機就叫做"a nonstop flight"，若是轉機班機則是"a stop-over flight"。

A : I'd like to book a nonstop flight from Taipei to New York.
我想預訂從台北到紐約的直達航班。

B : What time do you prefer?
您偏好什麼時間？

反義用法

例 I'd like to book a stop-over flight.
我要訂需要轉機的班機。

例 I'd like a stop-over flight to New York.
我要訂到紐約的轉機班機。

MP3 271

● 再確認機位
I'd like to reconfirm a flight.
我要再確認機位。

搭飛機之前，千萬要記得再一次確認你的班機。「確認班機」就叫做"reconfirm a flight"。

A：I'd like to reconfirm a flight.

我要再確認機位。

B：OK, sir. Your name, please.

好的，先生。請問您的大名？

相關用法

例 I'd like to reconfirm a flight for Mr. Smith.
我要替史密斯先生再確認機位。

MP3 272

● 取消機位
I'd like to cancel my reservation.
我想取消我的訂位。

當你預定機位後，若需要取消機位，則為"cancel th reservation"。

A：I'd like to cancel my reservation.

我想取消我的訂位。

B：OK, sir. May I have your name?

好的，先生。請問您的大名？

● 變更機位

I'd like to change my flight.

我想變更我的班機。

> 若需要變更班機,就要使用"change"這個字詞。最常用的表達方式就是"change the flight"。

A : I'd like to change my flight.

我想變更我的班機。

B : No problem, madam.

沒問題,女士。

● 辦理報到

Check-in, please.

我要辦理登機。

> "check"是個非常實用的字詞,特別是在辦理登記報到的時候,最常使用的句型就是"check in",例如搭機、飯店投宿等都適用。

A : Check-in, please.

我要辦理登機。

B : OK, sir. Passport and visa, please.

好的,先生。(請給我) 護照和簽證。

例 I'd like to check in.

我要辦理登機。

相關用法

例 Can I check in for CA Flight 861?
我可以辦理 CA861 班機登機嗎？

例 Where may I check in for United Airlines Flight 861?
我應該在哪裡辦理聯合航空 861 班機的登機手續？

例 What time should I have to be at the airport?
我應該什麼時候到機場？

 275

● 靠走道／靠窗的機位
May I have a window seat?
我可以要靠窗戶的座位嗎？

搭飛機坐選擇坐在窗戶旁或走道旁學問可大了，窗戶旁可以比較有隱密性、又有對外的透視感，而走道邊雖然感覺比較擁擠、得讓位給窗戶座位乘客通過，但是光是可以自由行動的便利性，就不得不犧牲一點隱私性囉！走道座位叫做"an aisle window"，窗戶座位則是"a window seat"。

A : May I have a window seat?
我可以要靠窗戶的座位嗎？

B : Sure, madam.
沒問題的，女士。

例 I don't want the aisle seat.
我不要靠走道的位子。

例 I want an aisle seat, please.
我想要一個靠走道的位子。

MP3 276

●行李托運
I have baggage to be checked.
我有行李要托運。

行李"baggage"主要是美式英語的說法，通常「一件行李」叫做"a piece of baggage"。而另一個常見的行李用法則為"luggage"，是為不可數名詞，沒有複數變化型。

A：I have baggage to be checked.
我有行李要托運。

B：Please put it on the scale.
請把它放在秤上。

例 I have two suitcases.
我有兩件行李箱。

相關用法

例 Can I carry this bag with me?
我可以隨身帶這個袋子嗎?

例 How many suitcases can I take on a China flight?
搭乘中國航空的班機我可帶多少件行李箱?

 277

●行李超重費用
How much is the extra charge?
超重費是多少?

> 每一家航空公司都有一定的行李搭載重量,萬一超過這個標準重量,可就要再付一筆超額費用"extra charge"。

A：How much is the extra charge?
超重費是多少?

B：You have to pay two hundred dollars for excess baggage.
那些超重的行李您要付兩百元。

同義用法

例 What are your charges for excess baggage?
你們的行李超重費是多少?

● 何處登機

Where should I board?

我應該到哪裡登機？

> "board"是登機的意思，可以泛指登上船、汽車或飛機等交通工具，例如"Flight 701 to Los Angeles is now boarding at gate 14A." （飛往洛杉磯的701航班即將在14A號登機門登機）而登機證就叫做"a boarding pass"。

A：Excuse me, where should I board?

請問，我應該到哪裡登機？

B：May I see your ticket?

給我看一下你的機票。

類似用法

例 Where is the boarding gate?

登機門在哪裡？

例 I don't know where I should board.

我不知道我應該在哪裡登機。

相關用法

例 I think I am at the wrong gate.

我想我走錯登機門了。

MP3 279

●轉機
How should I transfer?

我要如何轉機？

當需要轉乘另外一種交通工具到達目的地時，就需要使用"transfer"這個單字，例如"Simon transferred the car to his brother"。

A：How should I transfer?

我要如何轉機？

B：Let me see your ticket, please.

請給我看您的機票。

類似用法

例 How do I transfer to Washington?

我要如何轉機到華盛頓？

相關用法

例 Where can I get information on a connecting flight?

我可以到哪裡詢問轉機的事？

A：May I help you?

需要我協助的嗎？

B：Yes. Where can I get information on a connecting flight?

是的。我可以到哪裡詢問轉機的事？

● 行李提領

Where can I get my baggage?

我可以在哪裡提領我的行李?

> 出海關後,想到要提行李是不是就很傷腦筋?不用擔心,提領行李就叫做"get my baggage",而行李輸送帶則叫做"conveyer"。

A：Where can I get my baggage?

我可以在哪裡提領我的行李?

B：Your baggage is on the conveyer.

您的行李在行李傳輸帶上。

相關用法

例 Is this the baggage claim area from USA Airlines 561?

這是美國航空561班機的行李提領處嗎?

例 Can I get my baggage now?

我可以現在提領我的行李嗎?

例 Excuse me, sir, but that is my baggage.

先生,抱歉,那是我的行李。

例 Could you help me get my baggage down?

您可以幫我把我的行李拿下來嗎?

281

● 行李推車

Where can I get a baggage cart?

哪裡有行李推車？

若是你的行李數量很多或是重量很重，便少不了需要行李推車的協助，行李推車叫做"baggage cart"，而賣場中協助放置商品的推車則是"shopping cart"。

A：Where can I get a baggage cart?

哪裡有行李推車？

B：It's over there.

在那裡。

 282

● 行李遺失

I can't find my baggage.

我找不到我的行李。

搭飛機最怕行李遺失，若是需要告訴服務人員你找不到自己的行李，只要說："I can't find my baggage."就可以了！

A：I can't find my baggage. What can I do?

我找不到我的行李。我應該怎麼辦？

B：Don't worry about it.

不用擔心！

類似用法

例 I don't see my baggage.
我沒有看見我的行李。

例 One of my bags hasn't come.
我的一件行李沒有出來。

例 I think two pieces of my baggage have been lost.
我覺得我的兩件行李遺失了。

 283

● 行李遺失申報處

Where can I find the Lost Baggage Service?

我可以在哪裡找到行李遺失申報處？

行李遺失該怎麼辦？趕緊到機場設置的 "Lost Baggage Service"登記吧！

A：Where can I find the Lost Baggage Service?

我可以在哪裡找到行李遺失申報處？

B：It's over there.

在那裡。

同義用法

例 Do you know where the Lost Baggage Service is?
你知道行李遺失申報處在哪裡嗎？

MP3 284

● 兌換貨幣
Could you give me some small change with it?

您能把這些兌換為小面額零錢嗎？

> 若是要將大面額紙鈔「兌開」，是使用 "exchange" 或 "break"，而小面額的「零錢」，則叫做 "small change"。

A : Could you give me some small change with it?

您能把這些兌換為小面額零錢嗎？

B : How much would you like to exchange?

要換成多少？

同義用法

例 Would you please break this bill?
能請您將這張紙鈔找開嗎？

相關用法

例 Could you cash a traveler's check?
你可以把旅行支票換成現金嗎？

例 Where is the currency exchange?
貨幣兌換處在哪裡？

例 Can I exchange money here?
我可以在這裡兌換錢幣嗎？

● 查驗證件

This is my passport and visa.

這是我的護照和簽證。

"This is my..."是非常實用的句型,表示「這是我的…」,例如當海關人員要求檢驗相關的證件時,你就可以大方地說:"This is my passport and visa."

A:May I see your passport and visa, please?

請給我您的護照和簽證。

B:This is my passport and visa.

這是我的護照和簽證。

● 通關

Yes, I am alone.

是的,我一個人(來的)。

通關時,海關檢驗人員通常會問你是不是一個人來旅行,若你是單獨一個人,則表示是獨自前來的,就叫做"I am alone"。

A:Are you traveling alone?

您自己來旅遊的嗎?

B:Yes, I am alone.

是的,我一個人(來的)。

相關用法

例 I am with my parents.
我和我父母一起來的。

例 I am with a travel tour.
我是跟團的。

MP3 287

● 入境原因
It's for business.
(我)是來出差的。

入境的原因相當多種，最常見的當然就
是"for business"（出差）、"for sightseeing"（觀光）或是"for studies"（留學）。

A：What's the purpose of your visit?
您此行的目的是什麼？

B：It's for business.
(我)是來出差的。

相關用法

例 I am here for sightseeing.
我來這裡觀光。

例 I am here for studies.
我來這裡唸書的。

例 Just touring.
只是旅遊。

例 I am just passing through.
我只是過境。

●停留的時間

I'd stay here for two weeks.

我會在這裡停留兩個星期。

　　當海關詢問你停留在當地的時間，若是觀光行程，你只需要告知行程的天數即可，不用解釋太多，適用的句型為"stay here for ＋天數"。

A：How long are you going to stay?

　　您要停留多久？

B：I'd stay here for two weeks.

　　我會在這裡停留兩個星期。

類似用法

例 I'll stay here for one more week.

　　我會在這裡停留一個多星期。

例 It's about 3 weeks.

　　大概三個星期。

●隨身物品

Just personal belongings.

只是個人用品。

　　通關檢驗行李時，海關人員會對你所攜帶的物品做盤查，若沒有特殊需要說明的物品，你只要說"personal belongings"（個人用品）即可。

A：Why do you take them with you?

為什麼帶這些東西？

B：Just personal belongings.

只是個人用品。

同義用法

例 Personal stuff.

私人物品。

相關用法

例 They're just some souvenirs.

它們只是一些紀念品。

MP3 290

● 申報商品

I have nothing to declare.

我沒有要申報的物品。

> 攜帶某些商品超過一定數量就必須課稅，若是需要申報（declare）商品，就可以說 "I have... to declare"，表示「我有…要申報」。

A：Do you have anything to declare?

有沒有要申報的物品？

B：No, I have nothing to declare.

沒有，我沒有要申報的物品。

例 There are four bottles of wine to declare.
我有四瓶酒要申報。

 291

● 繳交稅款

How much is the duty on this?

這個要付多少稅金呢？

> 既然需要繳稅，就得知道「關稅」就叫做"duty"，需付關稅的商品則為"on＋物品"，例如"How much is the duty on the four bottles of wine?"（這四瓶紅酒要付多少關稅？）。

A：You have to pay duty on the excess.
您要付超重費。

B：How much is the duty on this?
這個要付多少稅金呢？

類似用法

例 How much is the duty?
稅金是多少？

例 How much did you say?
您說是多少？

相關用法

例 How should I pay for it?
我應該要如何付呢？

MP3 292

● 找不到座位

I couldn't find my seat.

我找不到我的座位。

> 和找不到行李的狀況很類似，利用"I coul-dn't find..."的句型，找不到座位時，就說："I couldn't find my seat."

A : I couldn't find my seat.

我找不到我的座位。

B : Let me see your ticket.

讓我看看您的機票。

MP3 293

● 尋求協助帶位

Would you please take me to my seat?

能請您幫我帶位嗎？

> 當你需要空服員（attendant）協助時，可以善用"Would you please..."的句型，說出："Would you please take me to my seat?"請對方帶領你就坐即可。

A : Would you please take me to my seat?

能請您幫我帶位嗎？

B : Down this aisle. It's on your right.

順著走道。就在您的右手邊。

同義用法

例 Could you show me where my seat is?
請問我的座位在哪裡？

(MP3) 294

● 確認座位號碼

My seat is 24M.

我的座位是 24M。

若是需要空服員帶領至座位上，除了提供登機證（boarding pass）給空服員看之外，也可以直接告訴空服員你的座位號碼。

A：My seat is 24M.

我的座位是 24M。

B：Go straight ahead, and you'll see it on your left.

往前直走，您就會看到在您的左手邊。

(MP3) 295

● 想要換座位

Can I change my seat?

我能不能換座位？

登機之後，若想要更換座位，必須等到飛機升空、解除不能隨意走動的限制後，才能向空服員提出更換座位（change seat）的要求。

A：Can I change my seat?

我能不能換座位？

B：I'm afraid not.

恐怕不行喔！

同義用法

例 Can you switch seats with me?

您能和我換座位嗎？

相關用法

例 Can we move to the smoking area?

我們能移到吸菸區嗎？

例 I'd like to move to the non-smoking area.

我想要換位子到非吸菸區。

 296

● 告知坐錯機位
That is my seat.

那是我的位子。

> 萬一你發覺已經有人坐在你的座位上時，
> 就可以客氣地告知對方："That's my seat."

A：Excuse me, but that is my seat.

抱歉，那是我的位子。

B：Sorry, my mistake.

抱歉，我坐錯了。

類似用法

例 I'm afraid this is my seat.

這個恐怕是我的座位。

例 I think 24M is my seat.

我覺得 24M 是我的座位。

●放行李

Where should I put my baggage?

我應該把我的行李放在哪裡？

上機之後，最重要的是行李的放置，除了隨身攜帶的重要證件袋之外，其他隨身的行李都需要放在頭頂上的行李置物櫃（the overhead cabinet）中，千萬不能放在走道上，以免影響飛安。

A : Excuse me. Where should I put my baggage?

請問一下，我應該把我的行李放在哪裡？

B : You can store extra baggage in the overhead cabinet.

您可以把多出來的行李放在上方的行李櫃裡。

相關用法

例 Would you please put this in the overhead bin for me?

您可以幫我把這個放進上方的櫃子裡嗎？

● 繫緊安全帶

How do I fasten my seat belt?

我要怎麼繫緊我的安全帶？

> 即將起飛（take off）之前，空服員一定會廣播"We will be taking off shortly. Please make sure that your seat belts are fastened." 要求乘客繫緊（fasten）安全帶（seat belt），並回到各自的座位，以等待起飛。

A：Excuse me, how do I fasten my seat belt?

請問一下，我要怎麼繫緊我的安全帶？

B：Let me show you.

我示範給您看。

● 盥洗室的方向

Where is the lavatory?

盥洗室在哪裡？

> 「上廁所」也是很重要的一件事，一定要先知道盥洗室的方向，並充分瞭解廁所門外的標誌："occupied"表示「廁所中有人正在使用」，而"vacant"則表示「廁所無人」。

A：Where is the lavatory?

盥洗室在哪裡？

B：Go straight ahead, and you'll see it on your right.

往前直走，您就會看到在您的右手邊。

●將椅背往後靠

Can I recline my seat back now?

我現在可以將我的椅背往後靠嗎？

若是你覺得椅背的斜度令人不舒服，則可以在飛機起飛之後，詢問空服員是否可以將椅背往後調整（**recline seat back**）。

A：Can I recline my seat back now?

我現在可以將我的椅背往後靠嗎？

B：Not now, sir.

現在不可以，先生。

●是否可以抽菸

May I smoke now?

我現在可以抽菸嗎？

雖然是在吸菸區，吸菸前還是問一下空服員你是否可以抽菸（**smoke**）。

A：May I smoke now?

我現在可以抽菸嗎？

B：Sorry, sir, this is non-smoking area.

抱歉，先生，這是非吸菸區。

MP3 302

●要求提供物品

May I have a blanket?

我能要一條毯子嗎？

> "May I have..."是一句非常實用的句型，適用在請求對方提供物品時使用。

A：I feel cold. May I have a blanket?

我覺得冷，我能要一條毯子嗎？

B：Sure. Would you also like a pillow?

好的。您需不需要枕頭呢？

相關用法

例 Do you have a Chinese newspaper?

你們有中文報紙嗎？

例 May I have a pack of playing cards?

可以給我一副撲克牌嗎？

例 May I have a headset?

可以給我一副耳機嗎？

例 May I have a glass of water?

可以給我一杯水嗎？

● 詢問用餐時間

What time will we have a meal served?

我們幾點會用餐？

通常「餐點」是需要服務人員提供的，所以才會使用被動句型"a meal served"，表示「提供餐點的服務」的意思。

A：Excuse me, what time will we have a meal served?

請問一下，我們幾點會用餐？

B：About 7 o'clock.

大約七點鐘。

● 提供哪些餐點選擇

What do you have?

你們有什麼（餐點）？

當空服員詢問你要何種餐點時，你就可以先詢問"What do you have?"表示「我不知道你們有什麼餐點，可以向我說明嗎？」的意思。

A：What would you like for dinner?

晚餐您想吃什麼？

B：What do you have?

你們有什麼（餐點）？

🎵 305

●選擇餐點

I'd like beef, please.

我要吃牛肉,謝謝。

若是空服員已經向你解釋提供何種餐點
選擇時,你就可以利用"I'd like ..."的句型。

A : What would you like for dinner?

晚餐您想吃什麼?

B : I'd like beef, please.

我要吃牛肉,謝謝。

相關用法

例 Do you have a vegetarian meal?

你們有素食餐點嗎?

例 Do you have instant noodles?

你們有泡麵嗎?

🎵 306

●選擇飲料

Coffee, please.

請給我咖啡。

和餐點一樣,直接說明你希望喝的飲料
名稱即可。

A : Coffee or tea?

咖啡或茶?

B : Coffee, please.

請給我咖啡。

A : How about you, sir?

先生，您呢？

C : No, thanks.

不用，謝謝！

●要求提供飲料

May I have a glass of water, please?

我能要一杯水嗎？

"a glass of..."表示「一杯…」的意思，通常可以適用此單位的飲料為果汁、白開水、酒類飲料等。

A : May I have a glass of water, please?

我能要一杯水嗎？

B : OK. I'll be right back with you.

好的。我馬上回來。

相關用法

例 May I have some more tea, please?

我能再多要點茶嗎？

例 Can I have some coffee?

我可以喝一些咖啡嗎？

例 May I have a glass of orange juice?

我能要一杯柳橙汁嗎？

例 May I have something to drink?

我能喝點飲料嗎？

308

● 飯店投宿

Do you have a twin-bedded room?

你們有兩張單人床的房間嗎？

投宿飯店時，記得要先告訴櫃臺人員你希望入住的房間規格，例如是單人房（a single room）或雙人房（a double room）等。

A：Do you have a twin-bedded room?

你們有兩張單人床的房間嗎？

B：Yes, we do.

是的，我們有。

相關用法

例 Do you have a single room?

你們有單人房嗎？

例 Do you have a double room?

你們有雙人床的房間嗎？

例 Do you have a twin available?

你們有兩張單人床的房間嗎？

A：Do you have a twin available?

你們有兩張單人床的房間嗎？

B：I'm sorry, sir, but we are all booked up.

抱歉，先生，我們全部客滿了。

● 飯店訂房

Do you have a twin available?

你們有兩張單人床的房間嗎？

雙人房（a double room）還分很多種，還有一種是兩張單人床所組合而成的雙人房間（a twin-bedded room）。"available" 表示是否還有空房的意思。

A：Do you have a twin available?

你們有兩張單人床的房間嗎？

B：No, but we have a double room available.

沒有，但是我們有一個雙人床房間。

A：OK. I will take it.

好，我要訂。

類似用法

例 I'd like a room for one.

我要一間單人房。

例 I'd like a room for two with separate beds.

我要一間有兩張床的雙人房間。

MP3 310

● 請求推薦旅館

Could you recommend another hotel?

可以幫我推薦另一間旅館嗎？

萬一旅館已經客滿，也可以問櫃臺人員附近是否有你可以投宿的旅館，以免你在人生地不熟的異國環境中拖著行李到處找旅館。不過還是建議您，出國前就先訂好房間，以免遇到旅館客滿的窘境。

A：Could you recommend another hotel?

可以幫我推薦另一間旅館嗎？

B：Yes. There is another hotel on First Street.

好的。在第一街有另一間旅館。

類似用法

例 Are there any hotels around here?

這附近還有沒有旅館？

MP3 311

● 詢問房價

How much per night?

一晚要多少錢？

前面提過了，只要詢問和價錢有關的訊息，都是使用"How much..."的訊息，本句不同的是，因為要詢問單一個夜晚的費用，所以可以再增加"per night"，以強調是詢問「一個晚上的住宿費用」。

A : How much per night?

　　一晚要多少錢？

B : It's eight hundred dollars per night.

　　一晚要八百元。

相關用法

例 How much for a single room?

　　單人房多少錢？

例 How much will it be?

　　要多少錢？

例 How much should I pay for a week?

　　一個星期得付多少錢？

例 Do you have any cheaper rooms?

　　你們有便宜一點的房間嗎？

 MP3 312

● 詢問房價包括的項目

Does the room rate include breakfast?

住宿費有包括早餐嗎？

「住宿費用」是"room rate"，通常你必須
要先確認此費用是否有包含早餐或其他的
項目費用，以免產生誤解。

A : Does the room rate include breakfast?

　　住宿費有包括早餐嗎？

B : Yes, sir.

　　有的，先生。

相關用法

例 Are there any meals included?

有包括餐點嗎？

例 Does it include tax?

有含稅嗎？

 313

● 登記住宿

I'd like to check in.

我要登記住宿。

和「登機報到」一樣，「登記住宿」也是使用"check in"這個片語。

A：May I help you, sir?

先生，有什麼需要我效勞的嗎？

B：I'd like to check in.

我要登記住宿。

MP3 314

● 何時可以登記住宿

When is the check-in time?

什麼時候可以登記住宿？

通常飯店的住宿報到是在下午三點鐘之後，萬一你提早到了當地，也可以試著詢問飯店是否可以提早讓你"check in"。

A：When is the check-in time?

什麼時候可以登記住宿？

B : Anytime after 11 am.

　　早上十一點鐘之後都可以。

類似用法

例 What time can I check in?

　　我什麼時候可以登記住宿？

 315

● 有預約訂房

I have a reservation.

我有預約訂房。

　若是要告訴飯店櫃臺你有預定房間，只
要簡單地說你有"reservation"即可，櫃臺
就會詢問你的大名（**May I have your
name?**），幫你辦理住宿手續。

A : Did you make a reservation?

　　您有預約住宿嗎？

B : Yes, I have a reservation. My name is Tom
Jones.

　　有的，我有預約訂房。我的名字是湯姆‧
瓊斯。

反義用法

例 No, I didn't make a reservation.
　　沒有，我沒有預約。

MP3 316

●房間的樓層
What's the floor?

在幾樓？

> 辦理好住宿登記後，櫃臺會將房間鑰匙
> 交給你，若是不知道樓層，就可以問對方
> **"What's the floor?"**（在幾樓？）

A：What's the floor?

在幾樓？

B：It's on the third floor.

在三樓。

MP3 317

●供餐
What time is breakfast served?

早餐什麼時候供應？

> 到飯店登記入住後，一定要記得問早餐
> 供應的時間，以免錯過用餐時間喔！

A：This is your breakfast coupon.

這是您的早餐券。

B：What time is breakfast served?

早餐什麼時候供應？

相關用法

例 Where should I go for the breakfast?

我應該去哪裡用早餐？

例 I forgot to bring breakfast coupons with me.

我忘了帶早餐券。

例 I lost my breakfast coupons.

我把早餐券弄丟了。

 318

● 表明身分

I'm Jack Smith of Room 705.

我是 705 號房的傑克・史密斯。

要告訴飯店櫃臺人員你的姓名或房號，以方便櫃臺人員提供協助。

A : What's your room number?

您的房號是幾號？

B : I'm Jack Smith of Room 705.

我是 705 號房的傑克・史密斯。

類似用法

例 This is Room 705.

這是 705 號房。

例 My room number is 705.

我的房間號碼是 705。

MP3 319

●領回代管的房間鑰匙

Room 705. Key, please.

房號 705。請給我鑰匙。

出門時，可以將房間鑰匙交由櫃臺人保
管，以免遺失鑰匙。要取回時，只需要簡
單報出房號即可。

A：Room 705. Key, please.

房號 705。請給我鑰匙。

B：Here you are, sir.

先生，在這裡。

類似用法

例 Key to Room 756, please.

我要拿房號 756 的鑰匙。

例 My room number is 756.

我的房間號碼是 756。

相關用法

例 I have lost my room key.

我弄丟房間鑰匙了。

MP3 320

●指明早上叫醒服務

Give me a wake-up call at 10.

在十點鐘打電話叫醒我。

請櫃臺人員早上定時叫你起床是非常棒
的服務，你可以多加利用。

A：Give me a wake-up call at 10, please.

請在十點鐘打電話叫醒我。

B：Yes, sir.

好的，先生。

類似用法

例 I'd like a wake-up call every morning.

我每一天都要早上叫醒(的服務)。

例 Could I have an early morning call, please?

我能有早上叫醒的服務嗎？

 321

●要求客房服務

I want a chicken sandwich.

我要一份雞肉三明治。

> 飯店中的「客房服務」（room service）
> 相當具有隱私性，若是你不想要下樓用餐，
> 只需點份餐點送到房間，侍者敲敲門就會
> 說" room service"，表示「餐點來囉！」

A：May I help you, sir?

先生，有什麼需要我效勞的嗎？

B：I want a chicken sandwich.

我要一份雞肉三明治。

相關用法

例 I'd like an extra pillow for Room 504.

我要在504房多加一個枕頭。

例 Would you bring us a bottle of champagne?

您能帶一瓶香檳給我們嗎？

例 I can't find any towels in my room.

我的房裡沒有毛巾。

例 Could you bring some towels right now?

請您馬上送幾條毛巾過來好嗎？

 322

●衣物送洗

Do you have laundry service?

你們有洗衣服務嗎？

> 出門在外最不方便的就是衣物的換洗，許多飯店都有"laundry service"的服務，也就是「衣物送洗」的服務，不妨多加利用！

A：Do you have laundry service?

你們有洗衣服務嗎？

B：Yes, we do. Please put it in the plastic bag and leave it on the bed.

有的，我們有。請放在塑膠袋裡，然後放在床上。

相關用法

例 I have some laundry.

我有一些衣服要送洗。

例 I'd like to send my suit to the cleaners.

我要把我的西裝送洗。

例 When can I have them returned?
我什麼時候可以取回他們？

> A：When can I have them returned?
> 我什麼時候可以取回他們？
> B：By this afternoon.
> 下午之前就可以。

MP3 323

● 撥打外線電話

How do I call a number outside this hotel?

我要怎麼從旅館撥外線出去？

若是你想要在飯店內撥打外線電話，通常在電話附近會有標示撥打外線的方法供你參考，或是你也可以直接打電話問櫃臺人員。

A：How do I call a number outside this hotel?
我要怎麼從旅館撥外線出去？

B：Dial 9 first, and then the phone number.
先撥九，再來是(撥)電話號碼。

相關用法

例 Is this coin all right for telephones?
這個硬幣可以打電話嗎？

例 Could you connect me with the telephone directory assistance?
可以幫我接查號台嗎？

259

324

●詢問退房時間

When is the check-out time?

退房的時間是什麼時候？

> 一般說來飯店的退房時間（check-out time）是在早上十一點鐘之前，但是建議你，在櫃臺登記入住時，還是要先問清楚退房時間。

A：When is the check-out time?

　　退房的時間是什麼時候？

B：Before 11 am.

　　早上十一點鐘之前。

 325

●辦理退房

I'd like to check out.

我要結帳。

> 在飯店要「退房」及「結帳」怎麼說？和反義用法「辦理登記入住」（check in）類似，就叫做"check out"。

A：I'd like to check out.

　　我要結帳。

B：Yes, sir.

　　好的，先生。

同義用法

例 Check out, please.

　　請結帳。

● 費用的多寡

How much does it cost?

這要收多少錢？

「這個賣多少？」除了最常見的"how much?"之外，也可以使用"How much does it cost?"來表示，這是比較正式的用法。 "cost"表示「索價」的意思。

A : How much does it cost?

這要收多少錢？

B : Your bill is twenty thousand dollars.

您的帳單是兩萬元。

相關用法

📕 Put it on my hotel bill, please.

請算在我的住宿費裡。

📕 Are there any additional charges?

是否有其他附加費用？

● 現金付款

I will pay cash.

我會付現金。

付款的時候，你可以告訴結帳人員，你要選擇用現金（cash）付款。

A：How would you like to pay it, sir?

先生，您要怎麼付錢呢？

B：I will pay cash.

我會付現金。

相關用法

例 By credit card.

用信用卡(付款)。

例 Can I pay with a traveler's check?

我可以用旅行支票付款嗎？

 328

●信用卡付款

Credit card, please.

我要用信用卡結帳。

除了現金付款之外，另一種常見的付款方式就是信用卡（**credit cards**）付款。

A：Cash or credit card?

用現金還是信用卡(付款)？

B：Credit card, please.

我要用信用卡結帳。

同義用法

例 Credit card. Here is my card.

信用卡。這是我的信用卡。

例 I'll pay it by credit card.

我要用信用卡結帳。

A：Would you pay it by cash or credit card?
　　您要用現金還是信用卡付款？
B：I'll pay it by credit card.
　　我要用信用卡結帳。

 329

● 帳單有問題

There is something wrong with the bill.

帳單有點問題。

「帳單」叫做"bill"，可不是人名「比爾」（Bill）的意思，當你覺得帳單的明細有問題時，一定要告訴結帳人員，請對方幫你再次確認帳單明細。

A：I'm afraid there is something wrong with the bill.
　　帳單恐怕有點問題。

B：Sorry, sir. Let me take a look.
　　抱歉，先生。我看一看。

相關用法

例 Are the service charges and tax included?
　　是否包括服務費和稅金？

263

生活句型
萬用手冊

MP3 330

● 和櫃臺互動

I'd like to change my room.

我想換房間。

入住飯店後，會有許多機會和櫃臺人員互動，他們通常會問："How may I help you?"你就可以直接說明你的需求。

A：How may I help you, sir?

先生，有什麼需要我效勞的嗎？

B：I'd like to change my room.

我想換房間。

相關用法

例 Where is the locker?

寄物櫃在哪裡？

例 Could you call a taxi for me, please?

請幫我叫部計程車好嗎？

MP3 331

● 是否有留言

Do I have any messages?

我有任何的留言嗎？

若是有朋友來拜訪你，恰巧你不在飯店，他們就可以請櫃臺人員代為轉達，你就可以問："Do I have any messages?"表示「我有任何的留言嗎？」

A：How may I help you, sir?

先生，有什麼需要我效勞的嗎？

B：Yes. Do I have any messages?

有的！我有任何的留言嗎？

類似用法

例 This is Tom Jones in Room 602. Do you have any messages for me?

我是602號房的湯姆·瓊斯。有沒有給我的留言？

 MP3 332

●房間反鎖

I locked myself out.

我把自己反鎖在外面了。

「將自己反鎖」要怎麼說？很簡單，就是"lock myself out"，舉凡反鎖在門外、車外等情況都適用。

A：How may I help you, sir?

先生，有什麼需要我效勞的嗎？

B：I locked myself out.

我把自己反鎖在外面了。

333

● 保管行李

Could you store my baggage?

請幫我保管行李好嗎？

請飯店櫃臺代為保管行李（store my baggage），可以讓你在退房之後，還有半天的時間可以安排短程觀光，而不必拖著笨重的行李到處跑。

A：Could you store my baggage?
請幫我保管行李好嗎？

B：Yes, of course.
好的。

相關用法

例 I'd like to pick up my baggage.
我要拿行李。

 334

● 詢問營業時間

When does the restaurant open?

餐廳幾點開始營業？

「商店營業時間」怎麼說？用白話的邏輯思考就是「商店開門營業時間」，只要用"open"就可以表示「開門營業」。

A：When does the restaurant open?
餐廳幾點開始營業？

B：The restaurant opens at 11 am.
餐廳早上十一點鐘開始營業。

● 打烊時間

How late are you open?

你們營業到幾點?

> "How late are you open?"表示「開門營業到多晚的時間」,也就是打烊的時間。

A : How late are you open?

你們營業到幾點?

B : We are open all night.

我們整晚都有營業。

同義用法

例 When does the restaurant close?

餐廳幾點打烊?

> A : When does the restaurant close?
>
> 餐廳幾點打烊?
>
> B : We are open until six thirty.
>
> 我們營業到六點卅分。

 336

● 建議餐點

Let's eat sandwiches for dinner.

我們晚餐吃三明治吧!

> 中文常說「我們去吃…」,常用句型就是"Let's eat...",若是是指「晚餐」則為"for dinner",而早、午餐則分為別"for breakfast"及"for lunch"。

A : What would you like for dinner?
　　您晚餐想吃什麼？

B : Let's eat noodles for dinner.
　　我們晚餐吃麵吧！

MP3 337

● 邀請用餐

Would you like to have dinner with us?

想和我們一起共進晚餐嗎？

用餐的動詞不一定非得用"eat"這個單字，例如「吃晚餐」就可以說"have dinner"來表示。一般說來，若是提出邀請，可以多多利用"Would you like to..."的句型。

A : Would you like to have dinner with us?
　　想和我們一起共進晚餐嗎？

B : We would love to, but we have other plans.
　　我們很想，但是我們有其他計畫。

MP3 338

● 隨便用餐

Let's grab something to eat!

我們隨便找點東西吃吧！

若是屬於「隨便吃以填飽肚子」，則可以使用"grab something to eat"的句型。

A : I am so hungry.
　　我好餓。

B : Let's grab something to eat!

我們隨便找點東西吃吧！

A : How about pizza? How do you say?

要不要吃披薩？你覺得呢？

相關用法

例 I'm not hungry at all.

我一點都不餓。

例 I want to try something different.

我想要試一試一些不一樣的。

例 I prefer to eat out.

我比較喜歡去外面用餐。

 339

● 餐廳訂位

I want to make a reservation.

我要訂位。

　　和預訂飛機的機位很類似，訂餐廳的位子也是使用"make a reservation"。

A : I want to make a reservation.

我要訂位。

B : What time, sir?

先生，(訂)什麼時間？

MP3 340

●已事先訂位

I made a reservation at seven.

我訂了七點鐘的位子。

> 除了說明自己已經"made a reservation"
> 之外,也可以順帶說明這是個預訂在七點
> 鐘的預約。

A：Did you have a reservation?

您有訂位了嗎?

B：Yes, I made a reservation at seven.

有的,我訂了七點鐘的位子。

類似用法

例 I had a reservation.
我已經有預約。

例 I made a reservation yesterday.
我昨天有訂位。

MP3 341

●訂位人數

I want a table for 2, please.

我要二個人的位子。

> 餐廳訂位除了"make a table"之外,
> 也可以直接說明"want a table"(要訂一張桌
> 位),也一併說明是「兩個人的位子」(for
> 2)。

A：Welcome to White House Restaurant.

歡迎光臨白宮餐廳。

B：I want a table for 2, please.

我要二個人的位子。

相關用法

例 I want to make a reservation for five people.

我想訂五個人的位子。

例 There are 4 of us.

我們有四個人。

例 How many persons, please?

請問有幾位？

> A：How many persons, please?
>
> 　請問有幾位？
>
> B：Four.
>
> 　四位。

MP3 342

● 說明用餐人數

There are 4 of us.

我們有四個人。

特地單獨說明訂位人數的用法，只要說明數量，或是利用句型"數量+ of us"，表示「我們有…人」，以達到說明用餐人數的用意。

A：For how many, please?

您要訂幾人(的位子)？

B：There are 4 of us.

我們有四個人。

類似用法

例 I am alone.

我一個人。

例 For 5.

五個人。

例 We are a group of 5.

我們有五個人。

例 A table for 4, please.

四個人的位子。

MP3 343

● 詢問餐廳是否客滿

Do you have a table available?

現在還有空位嗎？

"available"表示空閒、仍舊開放預約的意思。

A：May I help you?

需要我效勞嗎？

B：Do you have a table available?

現在還有空位嗎？

類似用法

例 Can we have a table?

有空位給我們嗎？

> A : Can we have a table?
> 　有空位給我們嗎？
> B : I'm sorry, but we are quite full tonight.
> 　很抱歉，今晚都客滿了。

● 餐廳已經客滿

It's booked up tonight.

今晚都客滿了。

> 若是餐廳「客滿」，則常用句型片語為
> "book up"。

A : Do you have a table available?

現在還有空位嗎？

B : It's booked up tonight.

今晚都客滿了。

同義用法

例 I'm afraid we are fully booked for tonight.
今晚的座位恐怕已訂滿了。

例 I'm afraid all our tables are taken.
恐怕我們所有的位子都坐滿了。

類似用法

例 There are no tables now.
現在沒有座位。

MP3 345

●等位子的時間
How long do we have to wait?

我們要等多久？

當你整晚等待空位有點不耐煩時，就可以詢問服務人員："How long do we have to wait?"表示你希望對方能提供說明。

A：Would you mind waiting until one is free?

您介意等到有空位嗎？

B：How long do we have to wait?

我們要等多久？

A：About thirty minutes, sir.

大概需要卅分鐘，先生。

MP3 346

●分開座位或併桌
Would you mind sitting separately?

各位介不介意分開坐？

也許餐廳客滿，只剩下必須分開坐的座位，當侍者這麼問的時候，你有權說你介意分開坐："I do mimd."

A：Would you mind sitting separately?

各位介不介意分開坐？

B：No, we don't mind.

不會，我們不介意。

例 Would you mind sharing a table?

您介不介意和其他人併桌?

MP3 347

●等待帶位

Are you being waited on, sir?

先生,有人為各位帶位嗎?

若是需要服務生帶位,表示你正在"wait on"。

A : Are you being waited on, sir?

先生,有人為各位帶位嗎?

B : No, we have been waiting here for 30 minutes.

沒有,我們已經在這裡等了卅分鐘了。

MP3 348

●吸菸/非吸菸區座位

Non-smoking, please.

(我要)非吸菸區。

餐廳服務生在安排位次時,一定會先確認「吸菸區」(smoking area)或「非菸區」(Non-smoking area)的需求。你只要說明是哪一種區域即可。

A : Where would you prefer to sit?

您喜歡坐哪裡?

B : Non-smoking, please.

(我要)非吸菸區。

反義用法

例 Smoking area. Thanks.

(我要)吸菸區。謝謝。

 349

● 願意等待座位安排

We can wait.

我們可以等。

若願意遵從餐廳的座位安排而等待，你就可以說"We can wait."

A : You have to wait for about 20 minutes for the non-smoking area.

要非吸菸區的話，你們大概要等廿分鐘。

B : That's all right. We can wait.

沒關係。我們可以等。

 350

● 服務生帶位

I'll show you to your table.

我來帶您入座。

當服務生要帶領你就座時，就會說；"I'll show you to your table."而另一種常見的說法則是："This way, please."

A : I'll show you to your table.

我來帶您入座。

B : Thanks.

謝謝！

例 This way, please.

這邊請。

例 Watch your step.

請小心腳步。

 351

● 已經有座位了

We have a table for you now.

我們現在有座位給您了。

既然先前詢問是否有空位，那麼當有座位時，服務生就會說："have a table for you now"。

A：How long do we have to wait?

我們要等多久？

B：I'm sorry to have kept you waiting. We have a table for you now.

抱歉讓您久等了。我們現在有座位給您了。

例 We're very sorry for the delay.

非常抱歉耽擱您的時間。

🎵 352

● 挑選座位的偏好

How about that seat at the corner?

角落的那個座位可以嗎？

"how about..."經常使用在詢問對方意見的情境，這裡是服務生詢問顧客是否滿意餐廳所安排的座位時使用。

A：Where would you prefer to sit, sir? How about that seat at the corner?

先生，您想坐哪裡？角落的那個座位可以嗎？

B：Not close to the gate.

不要離門口太近。

相關用法

例 By the window, please.
請給我靠窗的座位。

例 By the window, if you have.
如果有的話，(給我)靠窗的座位。

例 Just not close to the aisle.
只要不要靠近走道。

例 Far away from the rest room.
離盥洗室遠一點。

例 We'd like the seats near the window.
但是我們想要靠窗的座位。

> A : Please be seated.
>
> 請坐。
>
> B : But we'd like the seats near the window.
>
> 但是我們想要靠窗的座位。

 353

●不喜歡餐廳安排的座位
I don't like this area.

我不喜歡這一區。

> 若你不滿意所安排的座位，不妨直接告訴服務生你為何不喜歡這個座位。

A : How about this area?

這一區呢？

B : I don't like this area.

我不喜歡這一區。

類似用法

例 I don't like this seat. It's too cold here.

我不喜歡這個座位。這裡太冷了。

相關用法

例 I'd like a table on the side.

我想要靠邊的座位。

MP3 354

●指定座位

Could we take these two seats?

我們可以要這兩個座位嗎?

> 若是有中意的位子,則可以直接問服務生你希望能"take these seats",表示你希望能被安排在這個座位用餐。

A : Excuse me, could we take these two seats?

抱歉,我們可以要這兩個座位嗎?

B : Sure. Please be seated.

當然可以。請坐。

類似用法

例 May I take this seat?

我可以坐這個座位嗎?

例 May we have those two seats?

我們可以坐那兩個座位嗎?

MP3 355

●要求安靜的座位

Could we have a quiet table?

我們能不能選安靜的座位?

> 若是嫌位子太吵(too noisy)、太冷(too cold)或太熱(too hot),都可以請求服務生協助重新安排座位。

A : Could we have a quiet table?

我們能不能選安靜的座位?

B：I'll arrange another table for you immediately.

我馬上為您安排另一張桌子。

MP3 356

●沒有其他座位可以安排

We don't have other seats available.

我們沒有其他空位了。

若是沒有其他的空位可以重新安排，則你只能接受餐廳的安排了！

A：Is this fine with you?
這個(座位)好嗎？

B：We would like the seats near the window.
我們想要靠窗的座位。

A：I am sorry, sir, but we don't have other seats available.
很抱歉，先生，但是我們沒有其他空位了。

MP3 357

●要求提供開水

Would you please bring me a glass of water first?

能先幫我送一杯水來嗎？

當你就座後，就可以先請服務生提供一杯開水（a glass of water）給你。提供物品只要使用"bring me..."即可。

A : Please be seated, ladies and gentlemen.

請坐，各位先生女士。

B : Would you please bring me a glass of water first?

能先幫我送一杯水來嗎？

A : OK. I'll be right back with you.

好的。我馬上回來。

類似用法

例 May I have a glass of water?

我可以要一杯水嗎？

MP3 358

● 服務生隨後來點餐

I'll be right back for your order.

我待會馬上回來為您服務點餐。

服務生說明「馬上回來」通常使用"I'll be right back"，若是回來處理某事，則會加註說明，"for your order"表示「馬上回來服務點餐」。

A : Take your time. I'll be right back for your order.

慢慢來。我待會馬上回來為您服務點餐。

B : Thank you.

謝謝您。

類似用法

例 I'll be right back with you.

我待會馬上回來。

● 要求看菜單

May I see the menu, please?

請給我看菜單。

沒有什麼艱澀的單字，簡單提出你希望能先看一看菜單（see the menu）的要求。

A : May I see the menu, please?

請給我看菜單。

B : Sure. Here you are.

好的。請看。

360

● 還在看菜單

We are not ready to order now.

我們現在還沒有要點餐。

若是服務生詢問是否可以點餐，而你還在看菜單，就可以說："not ready to order"，希望他稍後再來點餐。

A : We are not ready to order now.

我們現在還沒有要點餐。

B : No problem. Take your time.

沒問題。您慢慢來。

類似用法

例 Can we order later?

我們可以等一下再點餐嗎？

📻 361

● 詢問是否要開始點餐

May I take your order?

您要點餐了嗎？

服務生詢問，「是否可以點餐」的萬用句型為"May I take your order?"字面意思「要拿你的點餐」就是表示「是否要開始點餐」或「點好餐了嗎」。

A：May I take your order?

您要點餐了嗎？

B：Yes, I'd like a turkey sandwich.

是的，我要一個火雞三明治。

類似用法

 Are you ready to order?

您準備好點餐了嗎？

> A：Are you ready to order?
>
> 您準備好點餐了嗎？
>
> B：We'll let you know if we are ready to order.
>
> 假使我們準備好要點餐，會讓你知道。

📻 362

● 點餐

I want to order Spaghetti.

我要點義大利麵。

點餐可以使用"I want to order ＋ 餐點"或是"I'd like to have ＋ 餐點"。

A：Ready to order now?

　準備好現在要點餐了嗎？

B：Yes, I want to order Spaghetti.

　是的，我要點義大利麵。

相關用法

例 I'll take the "A" course.

　我要 A 餐。

 363

● 尚未決定餐點

We have not decided yet.

我們還沒有決定。

> 還沒有點好餐或還在看菜單，就表示還沒有決定："have not decided"。

A：Are you ready to order?

　你們準備好點餐了嗎？

B：Sorry, we have not decided yet.

　對不起，我們還沒有決定。

類似用法

例 I haven't decided yet.

　我還沒有決定。

MP3 364

● 餐廳的特餐／招牌菜

What is today's special?

今天的特餐是什麼？

> 通常餐廳都會有招牌菜或今日特餐（to-day's special）的選擇，直接點這一種餐點就對了。

A：What is today's special?

今天的特餐是什麼？

B：It's Fillet Steak.

是菲力牛排。

類似用法

例 What's today's special of the house?
今天餐廳的特餐是什麼？

例 What's the specialty?
招牌菜是什麼？

例 What's the specialty of the restaurant?
餐廳的招牌菜是什麼？

MP3 365

● 推薦餐點

What would you recommend?

有什麼好的推薦嗎？

> 若是實在不知道該選擇哪一種餐點，不妨請服務生建議（recommend）吧！

A : What would you recommend?
　　有什麼好的推薦嗎？

B : The Spaghetti is the best one.
　　義大利麵是最棒的。

類似用法

例 What's your advice?
　　你的建議呢？

例 What is your suggestion?
　　你的建議呢？

 366

● 服務生徵詢推薦餐點

May I suggest something?

我能為您推薦一些(餐點)嗎？

　若是服務生很熱情，他們也是會主動提供熱門餐點的選擇。

A : May I suggest something?
　　我能為您推薦一些(餐點)嗎？

B : Please do if it's not bothering you.
　　如果不麻煩的話，請你推薦。

MP3 367

● 點服務生介紹的餐點

I'll try it.

我點這一個。

　若是你覺得服務生的建議聽起來不錯（sounds good），就可以嚐嚐看（I'll try it）喔！

287

A：You should try our sea food.

您應該要試試我們的海鮮。

B：It sounds good. I'll try it.

聽起來不錯。我點這一個。

同義用法

例 I'll try this one.

我要試這一種。

類似用法

例 I'll have Sirloin Steak and salmon for the lady.

我要點沙朗牛排，女士要(點)鮭魚。

相關用法

例 I have no idea about them.

我對這些不太清楚。

例 I like French cuisine.

我喜歡法式菜。

例 What do you have for Italian?

你們有哪些種類的義式餐點？

A：What kind of cuisine do you like? American or Italian?

您喜歡哪一種菜餚？美式或義式？

B：What do you have for Italian?

你們有哪些種類的義式餐點？

●前菜
What do you want for salad?

您要什麼沙拉？

> 正式的西餐通常會有前菜沙拉（salad），你得先選擇好喔！

A：What do you want for salad?

您要什麼沙拉？

B：I'd like the vegetable salad.

我要蔬菜沙拉。

●介紹沙拉
What salads do you have?

你們有什麼沙拉？

> 和"What do you have?"很類似，你也可以先問問服務生："What salads do you serve?"（你們有什麼沙拉？）

A：What salads do you serve?

你們有什麼沙拉？

B：We have Mixed Salad, Seafood Salad and Chef's Choice Salad.

我們有綜合沙拉、海鮮沙拉和主廚沙拉。

MP3 370

● 前菜醬料

Which kind of salad dressing

請問您要哪一種沙拉佐料？

> 沙拉點好了，不要忘記還有佐料（dressing）喔！

A：Which kind of salad dressing would you prefer?

請問您要哪一種沙拉佐料？

B：French, please.

請給我法式醬料。

C：I want Thousand Island.

我要千島醬。

MP3 371

● 點主菜

What do you want for the entrée?

您的正餐要點什麼？

> "I'd like to order + 餐點"是餐廳點餐中非常實用的句型，一定要記住！

A：What do you want for the entrée?

您的正餐要點什麼？

B：I'd like to order Sirloin Steak.

我要點沙朗牛排。

例 How about the meal?
(您的)正餐要點什麼？

例 What would you like for your main course?
主餐您要點什麼？

MP3 372

● 服務生詢問第二位點餐者
How about your order, madam?

女士，您要點什麼呢？

> 已經是在點餐的情境了，侍者問第二人之後的點餐，就可以直接問"How about you?"表示「您想點什麼？」

A：How about your order, madam?

女士，您要點什麼呢？

B：I will try Roast Chicken.

我要試試烤雞。

類似用法

例 And you, sir?
先生，您呢？

> A：And you, sir?
> 先生，您呢？
> B：Both of us would like Fillet Steak.
> 我們兩個都要菲力牛排。
> C：I'll have a mixed Salad and a Sirloin Steak.
> 我要一份綜合沙拉和一客沙朗牛排。

MP3 373

● 餐點售完

Sirloin Steak is sold out.

沙朗牛排賣完了。

商品「銷售一空」就叫做"be sold out"。

A：I'd like to order Sirloin Steak.

我要點沙朗牛排。

B：I'm sorry, but Sirloin Steak is sold out.

很抱歉，沙朗牛排賣完了。

類似用法

例 It's been sold out.

這道餐點已經賣完了。

例 It is not on the menu.

菜單上沒有這道菜。

例 Sirloin Steak is only available on weekends.

沙朗牛排只有在週末供應。

例 We don't have New York Steak now.

我們現在沒有紐約牛排。

> A：I'd like to order New York Steak.
> 我要點紐約牛排。
> B：I'm sorry, sir, but we don't have New York Steak now.
> 先生，很抱歉，但是我們現在沒有紐約牛排。

● 詢問餐點配方

What kind of dish is it?

這是什麼菜？

> 若是對主餐的內容有任何的疑問，"What kind of dish is it?"是非常實用的問句，服務生會解答你的疑問。

A：What kind of dish is it?

這是什麼菜？

B：It's American seafood marinated in lemon juice and chili peppers.

這是美式海鮮，用檸檬汁和胡椒醃漬。

同義用法

例 What is the recipe?

這是什麼配方？

> A：What is the recipe?
> 這是什麼配方？
> B：It's beef stewed in red wine.
> 那是用紅酒燉煮的牛肉。

相關用法

例 Do you serve beefsteak pie with gravy?

你們有供應有肉汁的牛排派嗎？

● 點和其他客人相同餐點

I'll have the same.

我點一樣的。

> 直接表明要點和同桌的前一個點餐者相同餐點，就可以直接說"the same"，表示「要一樣的餐點」。

A：I'd like Sirloin Steak, please.

我要點沙朗牛排，謝謝！

B：How about you, sir?

先生，您呢？

C：I'll have the same.

我點一樣的。

類似用法

例 We'd like this course for two, please.

這道菜請給我們來兩人份的。

例 Make it two.

點兩份。

> A：May I have your order now?
>
> 您要餐點了嗎？
>
> B：Yes, I'd like to order an apple pie.
>
> 好的，我要點一份蘋果派。
>
> A：How about you, madam?
>
> 您呢，女士？
>
> C：Make it two.
>
> 點兩份！

● 指明要點相同餐點

Can I have the same as that?

我能點和那個一樣的(餐點)嗎？

> 其他人點的餐點，你也同樣有興趣，就可以不必說一樣的餐點名稱，只要指著對方的餐點說"Can I have the same as that"就可以了！

A：May I take your order now?

我可以幫您點餐了嗎？

B：Can I have the same as that?

我能點和那個一樣的(餐點)嗎？

同義用法

例 Same here.

我也是點相同的餐點。

例 I'm going to order the same thing.

我要點一樣的餐。

例 I'll have that, too.

我也要那個。

MP3 377

● 是否還要點餐

And what would you like after that?

在這個之後您要點什麼？

> 點完一道餐點後，服務生會再次確認你
> 是否還有其他餐點需要點選："What would
> you like after that?"以確認是否完成餐點。

A：And what would you like after that?

在這個之後您要點什麼？

B：Then I want some pizza, too.

然後我還要披薩。

MP3 378

● 牛排烹調的熟度

Well done, please.

請給我全熟。

> 牛排的烹調熟度會影響牛排的口感，點
> 牛排時千萬記得要告訴侍者你的選擇：well
> done（全熟）、medium（五分熟）、me-
> dium rare（四分熟）、rare（三分熟）。

A：How would you like your steak cooked?

您的牛排要幾分熟？

B：Well done, please.

請給我全熟。

相關用法

例 Medium, please.
請給我五分熟。

例 Medium rare, please.
請給我四分熟。

例 Rare, please.
請給我三分熟。

●副餐餐點

Which vegetables come with the steak?

牛排的副餐是什麼?

若是你想要知道主餐的副餐蔬菜,就可以問"Which vegetables come with the steak?"

A:Which vegetables come with the steak?
牛排的副餐是什麼?

B:Onion rings and noodles.
洋蔥圈和麵。

類似用法

例 What do you serve?
你們有供應哪些?

相關用法

例 This dish contains fried eggs and vegetables.
這道餐有煎蛋和蔬菜。

例 There are several side dishes.
有許多種副餐。

MP3 380

● 湯點
We have both clear soup and thick soup.
我們清湯和濃湯都有。

湯點也是很重要的選擇，不要忘記也同
樣可以使用"I want to try..."的句型。

A：We have both clear soup and thick soup.
我們清湯和濃湯都有。

B：I want to try seafood soup.
我要試一試海鮮湯。

MP3 381

● 甜點／麵包種類
I want some cookies, please.
我要一些餅乾。

麵包的選擇相當多，侍者會問你「要哪
一種麵包」"What kind of bread."

A：What kind of bread do you want?
您要哪一種麵包？

B：I want some cookies, please.
我要一些餅乾。

同義用法

例 I'll try ice cream.
　　我要點冰淇淋。

例 I want to have chocolate cake.
　　我要點巧克力蛋糕。

例 I want pudding.
　　我要布丁。

> A：After the meal, what would you like for
> 　　dessert?
> 　　正餐後，您要什麼甜點？
> B：I want pudding.
> 　　我要布丁。

 382

● 要求再提供甜點
Would you bring us some bread?

您能再給我們一些麵包嗎？

> 若是希望餐廳能再提供甜點，就請服務
> 生拿一些（**bring us some...**）過來吧！

A：Would you bring us some bread?
　　您能再給我們一些麵包嗎？
B：Yes, I'll be right back.
　　好的，我馬上回來。

相關用法

例 I want some too, please.
　　我也要一些。

例 Please give me another sandwich.
請再給我另一份三明治。

MP3 383

● 詢問是否要點飲料
Would you like something to drink?
您要不要來點飲料？

"Would you like something to drink?"這是
一句非常普通的問句，不但適合餐廳點餐，
也適合問來訪的訪客想喝點什麼飲料。

A：Would you like something to drink?
您要不要來點飲料？

B：Sure. I want something cold.
好啊！我想要喝點冷飲。

類似用法

例 Anything to drink?
飲料呢？

相關用法

例 Which would you prefer, tea or coffee?
您要茶還是咖啡？

例 Would you like to order some wine with
your meal?
您想不想點酒搭配您的餐點？

● 點酒類飲料

I'd like the brandy.

我要白蘭地酒。

> 點餐另一種常用句型則為"I'd like + 餐點"，
> 表示「我要點選某餐點」。

A : What kind of alcohol do you want?

　　您要喝什麼酒？

B : I'd like the brandy.

　　我要白蘭地酒。

同義用法

例 Brandy, please.

　　請給我白蘭地。

相關用法

例 Beer is fine.

　　啤酒就好。

● 喜歡服務生推薦的飲料

It sounds terrific. I'll take it.

聽起來很棒。我就點這個。

> 同樣地，希望侍者能提供餐點建議時，
> 就可以問"What is your suggestion?"若是
> 覺得侍者所推薦的餐點合你的意，就可以
> 說 "It sounds terrific."

A：What is your suggestion for drinks?

你對飲料的建議是什麼？

B：We have brandy and beer.

我們有白蘭地和啤酒。

A：It sounds terrific. I'll take it.

聽起來很棒。我就點這個。

同義用法

例 Interesting. I'll take it.

很有趣。我就點這個。

例 Coffee would be fine.

就點咖啡。

MP3 386

● 要求再提供飲料

May I have some more wine, please?

我能再多要一些酒嗎？

若是飲料喝完了該怎麼？就可以說"May I have some more + 飲料?"，請侍者能多提供一些飲料。

A：May I have some more wine, please?

我能再多要一些酒嗎？

B：OK. I'll be right back with you.

好的。我馬上回來。

● 詢問是否完成點餐
Is that all for your order?

您點的就這些嗎?

> 當顧客點完餐點後,服務生都會順帶問一句"Is that all for order?"表示詢問是否都已經點完餐點了?是否需要再額外點餐。

A : Is that all for your order?

您點的就這些嗎?

B : That's all for us. Thank you.

我們就點這些。謝謝你!

同義用法

例 Will that be all?

就這樣?

類似用法

例 Anything else?

還有沒有要其他(餐點)?

例 What else are you going to have?

您還要點什麼嗎?

例 Is there anything else?

還要不要別的?

MP3 388

● 催促盡快送上餐點
Could you serve us quickly?

能不能快一點為我們上菜？

> 若是等了很久餐點還是沒有上，就應該要求服務生"Could you serve us quickly?"讓廚房能快一點上菜。

A：Could you serve us quickly?
　　能不能快一點為我們上菜？

B：No problem, sir.
　　先生，沒問題。

相關用法

例 Why is my steak taking so long?
　　為什麼我的牛排要這麼久？

MP3 389

● 請同桌者遞調味料
Please pass me the salt.

請遞給我鹽。

> 西餐禮儀中，切忌用手橫過同桌者面前取物或餐點，你可以請同桌者遞（pass）給你。

A：Excuse me, please pass me the salt.
　　對不起，請遞給我鹽。

B：Sure, here you are.
　　好的，給您。

●提供物品給對方
Here you are.

給你。

當你拿某個物品給對方時，就可以說"
Here you are."類似中文的口語「在這裡，
拿去」的意思。

A：Here you are.

給你。

B：What for?

為什麼要給我？

A：For good luck.

祝你好運啊！

●同意服務生上菜
Yes, please.

好的，請便。

若是服務生問你是否可以上菜（serve
your meal）時，你就可以說："Yes, please"，表示「請便」的意思。

A：May I serve your meal now?

現在可以上您的餐點嗎？

B：Yes, please.

好的，請便。

相關用法

例 May I serve your soup now?
我現在可以上您的湯點嗎？

例 May I serve coffee now?
我現在可以上咖啡嗎？

例 May I serve it to you now?
我現在可以幫您上菜了嗎？

 392

●服務生送錯餐點
This is not what I ordered.

這不是我點的餐點。

當發覺服務生送錯餐點時，就得馬上反應：**"This is not what I ordered."**

A：This is not what I ordered.
這不是我點的餐點。

B：Sorry, sir. I'll check your order right now.
抱歉，先生。我馬上確認您的餐點。

 393

●少送餐點
Is there a dish missing?

是不是少送一道餐點？

miss 表示「失蹤」，也可以表示「有餐點少送」的意思。

A : Is there a dish missing?

　是不是少送一道餐點？

B : Let me check your order.

　讓我確認您的餐點。

相關用法

例 I'm afraid there is a dish missing.

　恐怕有一道餐點沒來。

類似用法

例 Where are my onion rings?

　我的洋蔥圈呢？

 394

●主餐醬料

What would you like for the dressing?

您要哪一種醬料？

> 許多牛排都會搭配醬料，服務生上牛排後，都會確定你希望提供的醬料："for the dressing"。

A : What would you like for the dressing?

　您要哪一種醬料？

B : Black pepper, please.

　請給我黑胡椒。

相關用法

例 I'll take both kinds of steak sauce.

　兩種牛排醬料我都要。

> A：How about you, sir?
> 　　先生，您呢？
> B：I'll take both kinds of steak sauce.
> 　　兩種牛排醬料我都要。

MP3 395

●茶的濃與淡
Strong, please.
請給我濃的。

> 茶的濃淡是用"strong"和"weak"表示。

A：Do you take your tea strong or weak?
　　您喝濃茶還是淡茶呢？

B：Strong, please.
　　請給我濃的。

同義用法

例 I'd like my tea sweet.
　　我喝茶喜歡放糖。

MP3 396

●加奶精
I don't take milk with my coffee.
我喝咖啡不加牛奶。

> 將奶精加入咖啡中，只要說"take milk with coffee"即可。

A：Do you take it with milk?
　　您要不要加牛奶？

B：No, I don't take milk with my coffee.

不用，我咖啡不加牛奶。

 397

● 飲料加糖

How many lumps of sugar?

要加幾塊糖？

> 飲料中加的方糖，使用單位是"lump"，所以問對方要加幾給顆方糖就是用"How many lumps of sugar?"

A：How many lumps of sugar?

要加幾塊糖？

B：Two, please.

請給我兩塊。

反義用法

例 I don't put sugar into my coffee.

我喝咖啡不加糖。

398

● 飲料續杯

May I have a refill?

我可以續杯嗎？

> "refill"表示再加滿一杯的意思，通常就是表示「續杯」的意思。

A：May I have a refill?

我可以續杯嗎？

B：Of course, sir.

當然可以，先生。

類似用法

例 May I have some more coffee?

我能多要一些咖啡嗎？

 399

● 要求服務生提供協助

Could you bring us a few napkins?

可以給我們一些紙巾嗎？

和希望服務生提供麵包的句型類似，都是使用："Could you bring us + 物品"。

A：Can I get you anything else?

各位還需要其他東西嗎？

B：Well, could you bring us a few napkins?

嗯，您可以給我們一些紙巾嗎？

相關用法

例 Would you bring us a high chair for her?

可以幫我們拿一張兒童椅給她嗎？

例 May I have more napkins?

能給我多一點紙巾嗎？

例 Can you bring me the ketchup?

請拿蕃茄醬來好嗎？

例 Please bring me the mustard?

請拿芥末給我好嗎？

例 Can we have another chair?
我們能再要一張椅子嗎？

MP3 400

● 呼叫服務生

Excuse me.

服務生，請過來！

"Excuse me"不但適用在招呼服務生過來、注意之外，也適用在請對方讓路借過的情境中，有「抱歉打擾」的意思。

A：Excuse me.
　　服務生，請過來！

B：Yes, sir, may I help you?
　　是的，先生，需要我的協助嗎？

相關用法

例 Waiter.
男服務生。

例 Waitress.
女服務生。

MP3 401

● 更換餐具

May I have a new one?

我能要一支新的嗎？

希望服務生能夠更換新的餐具，只要使用"have a new one"的句型就可以了！

A：I dropped my fork. May I have a new one?
　　我的叉子掉到地上了，我能要一支新的
　　嗎？

B：Of course, sir. I'll change a new one for
　　you.
　　可以的，先生。我會幫您換支新的。

類似用法

例 This spoon is a little dirty.
　　這支湯匙有一點髒。

例 I dropped my spoon on the floor.
　　我的湯匙掉在地上了。

例 This glass is cracked!
　　這個玻璃杯有裂痕！

例 My plate is chipped!
　　我的盤子有缺口！

> A：Waiter! My plate is chipped!
> 　　服務生！我的盤子有缺口！
> B：Sure. I'll be right back.
> 　　好的。我馬上回來。

MP3 402

● 整理桌面

Would you clear the table for us?

您可以為我們整理一下桌子嗎？

> 在高級餐廳中用完餐之後，服務生就有
> 義務馬上清理桌面（clear the table），千
> 萬不要以為服務生在趕人結帳喔！

A：Would you clear the table for us?

您可以為我們整理一下桌子嗎？

B：Yes, sir.

好的，先生。

相關用法

例 I'm still working on it.

我還在用餐。

例 Yes, please, Oh...leave that left.

好的，謝謝！喔…那個留下來。

A：May I clear your table?
　　需要我幫您清理桌面嗎？

B：Leave that left.
　　那個留下來。

MP3 403

●已經用完餐點

We have finished it.

我們用完餐了。

　服務生清理桌面時，若是服務生問你是否仍在用餐，你就可以告知："We have finished it.（我們用完餐了）。

A：Have you finished or still working on it?

您用完餐或是還要繼續用餐？

B：We have finished it.

我們用完餐了。

MP3 404

● 答應收回餐盤
Please. Thank you.
麻煩您。謝謝。

服務生清理桌面時，會先問你是否可以收拾餐盤，你可以簡短地回答："Please. Thank you."表示「麻煩你收拾餐盤」的意思。

A：May I take your plate?
　　我可以收走您的盤子了嗎？

B：Please. Thank you.
　　麻煩您。謝謝。

類似用法

例 Sure, go ahead.
　　好的，請便。

MP3 405

● 向餐廳抱怨餐點
The milk is sour.
牛奶發酸了。

若是你對餐點不滿意，一定要馬上向服務人員反映，千萬不要當冤大頭喔！

A：May I help you?
　　有什麼需要我協助的嗎？

B：The milk is sour.
牛奶發酸了。

類似用法

例 This food tastes strange.
這道食物嚐起來味道很怪！

例 It's too oily.
太油膩了。

例 This is tough.
（肉質）好硬啊！

例 The meat is overdone.
肉煮太熟了。

例 The toast is too dark!
吐司烤得太焦了！

例 My steak is too rare.
我的牛排太生了。

例 There's an insect in my salad!
我的沙拉裏有蟲！

例 There is a hair in my soup!
我的湯裏有根頭髮！

相關用法

例 The food is getting cold.
食物變涼了。

例 Can you take it back and cook it longer?
請拿回去再烤久一點好嗎？

MP3 406

●分開結帳

Do you want separate checks?

你們要不要分開付帳？

> 若是一群人一起用餐，細心的服務生會問你是否需要分開結帳，以免一群人在餐廳門口拆帳，會顯得失去禮儀。

A：Do you want separate checks?

你們要不要分開付帳？

B：OK.

好的。

類似用法

⑳ Would you like to separate your checks?

各位要分開您的帳單嗎？

MP3 407

●請喝飲料

Let me buy you a drink.

我請你喝一杯。

> 在酒吧中常常會有請喝飲料的情境，這種「我請你喝一杯」就叫做"buy you a drink"。

A：By the way, my name is Judy.

對了，我是茱蒂。

B：Hi, I'm David. Let me buy you a drink.

我是大衛，讓我請你喝一杯。

例 I will buy you a drink today.
今天我請你喝一杯。

MP3 408

● 各自付帳
Let's go Dutch.
我們各付各的！

> 為了不要佔對方便宜，就可以分開結帳，甚至說讓我們各付各的費用，就叫做"go Dutch"。

A：Let me buy you a drink.
　　我請你喝一杯。

B：OK, but let's go Dutch.
　　好啊，但是我們各付各的吧！

相關用法

例 Let's go Dutch for dinner.
晚餐我們各付各的。

例 It's my treat this time.
這次我請客。

> A：It's my treat this time.
> 　　這次我請客。
> B：OK, if you insist.
> 　　好啊！如果你堅持。
> A：Sure. What do you want to have?
> 　　當然！你想吃什麼？

●不必找零
Keep the change.

不用找零錢了。

> "Keep the change"是很大方的行為，「不必找零錢」另一層意思就等於是付出一筆不限金額、隨意的服務費。

A：Here is 100 dollars.
這是一百元。

B：Here is your receipt and change.
這是您的收據和零錢。

A：Keep the change.
不用找零錢了。

●速食店點餐
I'll have a small fries.

我要一份小薯條。

> 點餐除了前面的"order"之外，也常用"I'll have + 餐點"表示。

A：I'll have a small fries.
我要一份小薯條。

B：Here is your order.
這是您的餐點。

相關用法

> 例 I'll have a Big Mac.
> 我要一個麥香堡。

例 I'll have a hamburger with a lot of ketchup.
我要點一個漢堡，要有很多蕃茄醬。

MP3 411

● 內用或外帶
For here, please.

內用，麻煩您。

速食店點餐最常聽見的問句就是內用或外帶（Stay or to go?），若是要內用，則可以說："For here, please."就可以了，而要外帶，則說"To go, please."

A：For here or to go?

要這裏用還是外帶？

B：For here, please.

內用，麻煩您。

相關用法

例 That'll be for here.
要在這裡吃。

例 To go, please.
帶走，麻煩你。

MP3 412

● 添加醬料
Would you like anything on it?

您要加什麼在上面嗎？

這裡所添加的醬料，多半是指加在漢堡或熱狗等餐點上。

A : Would you like anything on it?

您要加什麼在上面嗎？

B : Yes, cheese and a lot of mustard.

好的，要起司和很多芥末。

相關用法

例 Butter, please.

請給我奶油。

例 Make it honey.

要蜂蜜口味的。

MP3 413

● 多要一些醬料
Can I have extra ketchup?

我能多要蕃茄醬嗎？

希望服務生能再多提供蕃茄醬就叫做
"have extra ketchup"，也可以是胡椒粉、
糖、奶精等。

A : Can I have extra ketchup?

我能多要蕃茄醬嗎？

B : Sure. Here you are.

當然可以。這是您要的。

● 說明糖包和奶精的量

Two sugars and two creams, please.

請給我兩包糖和兩包奶精。

"two sugars, please"的句子，是直接告知服務生你所需要的糖和奶精數量即可。

A : Cream or sugar?

要奶精還是糖？

B : Two sugars and two creams, please.

請給我兩包糖和兩包奶精。

類似用法

例 Two sugars and no cream.

糖兩包，不要奶精。

例 Just cream, please.

請給我奶精就好。

● 只看不買的逛街

I'm just looking.

我只是隨便看看。

逛街常常都只是看看櫥窗商品，而不買商品，這種逛街就叫做"window shopping"。

A : May I help you with something?

需要我幫忙的嗎？

B：No. I'm just looking.

　　不用。我只是隨便看看。

相關用法

例 No. Thanks.

　　不用。謝謝！

例 Maybe later. Thank you.

　　也許等一下要（麻煩你），謝謝。

例 I don't need any help.

　　我不需要任何服務。

例 Not yet. Thanks.

　　還不需要。謝謝！

MP3 416

● 找商品

I'm looking for some gifts for my kids.

我在找一些要送給孩子們的禮物。

「尋找」的片語叫做"look for"，也適用在逛街尋找商品時使用。

A：I'm looking for some gifts for my kids.

　　我在找一些要送給孩子們的禮物。

B：Is there anything special in mind?

　　心裡有想好要什麼嗎？

相關用法

例 Are there any souvenirs made in the USA?

　　有沒有美國製造的紀念品？

MP3 417

● 購買禮品

It's for my daughter.

是給我女兒的。

> 表示所購物的商品是給某人的禮物,就
> 叫做"It's for + 某人"。

A : Is it a present for someone?

是送給誰的禮物嗎?

B : Yes, it's for my daughter.

是的,是給我女兒的。

MP3 418

● 購買特定商品

I want to buy the earrings.

我想要買耳環。

> "I want to buy + 物品",直接點名所要購
> 買(buy)的商品名稱。

A : What do you want to buy?

您想買什麼?

B : I want to buy the earrings.

我想要買耳環。

類似用法

例 I need a pair of gloves.

我需要手套。

例 I'm looking for some skirts.

我正在找一些裙子。

例 Do you have any purple hats?
你們有賣紫色的帽子嗎？

例 Do you have any hats like this one?
你們有沒有像這類的帽子？

MP3 419

● 檢視商品
I'd like to see some ties.
我想看一些領帶。

> 「檢視商品」的動詞非常多種，可以使用"see"或是"have a look"等。

A：What would you like to see?
您想看些什麼？

B：I'd like to see some ties.
我想看一些領帶。

相關用法

例 May I see those MP3 players?
我能看那些 MP3 播放器嗎？

例 May I have a look at them?
我能看一看它們嗎？

例 Can you show me something different?
您能給我看一些不一樣的嗎？

例 Show me that pen.
給我看那支筆。

例 Please show me that black sweater.
請給我看看那件黑色毛衣。

> A : Which one do you like?
>   您喜歡哪一件？
> B : Please show me that black sweater.
>   請給我看看那件黑色毛衣。

MP3 420

●找到中意的商品
I'm interested in this computer.
我對這台電腦有興趣。

> 當你對某商品感到有興趣時，就可以使用"I'm interested in + 商品"的句型。小心喔，是"interested"而不是"interesting"，兩者是不同的。

A : Did you find something you like?
    找到您喜歡的東西了嗎？
B : Yes, I'm interested in this computer.
    對，我對這台電腦有興趣。

類似用法

例 It looks nice.
    這個看起來不錯。

MP3 421

●新品上市
They are new arrivals.
他們都是新品。

> 「新品上市」英文就叫做"new arrival"，字面意思是「初抵達」，也就是表示是「新到貨的商品」。

A：They are new arrivals.

他們都是新品。

B：Can I pick it up?

我可以拿起來(看看)嗎？

 422

●特定顏色

Do you have any ones in blue?

你們有藍色的嗎？

> 若是要說明某商品是否有某種顏色時，是使用"in＋顏色"，例如："Do you have this any ones in blue?"

A：What color do you like?

您想要哪一個顏色？

B：Do you have any ones in blue?

你們有藍色的嗎？

相關用法

例 I'm looking for a pair of blue socks.

我在找藍色的襪子。

例 Both red and blue are OK.

紅色或藍色都可以。

例 Do you have this size in any other colors?

有這個尺寸的其他顏色嗎？

● 選擇顏色

I prefer blue.

我喜歡藍色。

"prefer"是「偏好」的意思，後面可以加名詞或動名詞，適合使用在任何的場合中，例如"I prefer living abroad."(我偏好住在海外)

A：I prefer blue.

我喜歡藍色。

B：OK. Let me show you some blue skirts.

好的。讓我拿一些藍色的裙子給您看。

相關用法

㊟ We only have red ones.

我們只有紅色。

㊟ We are out of blue, sir.

先生，我們沒有藍色。

㊟ Would you like to see black ones?

您要看看黑色的嗎？

● 尺寸說明

My size is 8.

我的尺寸是八號。

買衣物最重要的就是尺寸，你必須清楚地讓銷售人員知道你的尺寸，所以請善用"my size is..."的句型。

A：What is your size?

您的尺寸是多少？

B：My size is 8.

我的尺寸是八號。

同義用法

例 Give me size 8.

給我八號。

相關用法

例 My size is between 8 and 7.

我的尺寸是介於八號和七號之間。

例 I want the large size.

我要大尺寸的。

例 I will try on a small.

我要試穿小號的。

例 It's a small and I wear a medium.

這是小號的，而我穿中號的。

例 Size 8 in black.

(給我)黑色的八號尺寸。

例 It's not the right size.

尺寸不對。

例 I don't know my size.

我不知道我的尺寸。

> A : What size do you want?
>
> 您要什麼尺寸？
>
> B : I don't know my size.
>
> 我不知道我的尺寸。
>
> A : I can measure you up.
>
> 我可以幫您量。

 425

●詢問提供哪些尺寸

What sizes do you have?

你們有什麼尺寸？

> 若是你沒有非常確認適穿的尺寸，就可以詢問銷售人員有哪些尺寸選擇。

A : What sizes do you have?

你們有什麼尺寸？

B : This comes in several sizes.

這有好多種尺寸。

相關用法

例 Do you have this one in small?

你們有這一種小號的嗎？

 426

●量尺寸

Let me measure your waist.

我幫您量腰圍。

> 若是你不知道自己的尺寸，可以請銷售人員幫你丈量"please measure my waist"。

A：I don't know what my size is.

我不知道我的尺寸。

B：Let me measure your waist.

我幫您量腰圍。

同義用法

例 I can measure you for your suit.

我可以幫您量西裝。

相關用法

例 It's size 32, right?

是 32 號，對嗎？

例 Your size is 8, I guess.

我猜您的尺寸是八號。

MP3 427

● 要求試穿

Can I try this on?

我可以試穿這一件嗎？

「試穿」的片語是"try on"，若是你希望能夠試穿衣物，就可以問問銷售人員"Can I try this on?"（我可以試穿這一件嗎？）

A：Can I try this on?

我可以試穿這一件嗎？

B：Sure. This way please.

好啊。這邊請。

類似用法

例 May I try on that one, too?
我也可以試穿那一件嗎？

相關用法

例 Your're not allowed to try it on.
不可以試穿。

 428

●試穿特定尺寸
Could I try a larger one?
我可以試穿大一點的嗎？

> 若是試穿的結果不滿意，你可以告訴銷
> 售人員是太大（too large）或太小（too
> samll）等。

A：How about this size?

這一個尺寸如何？

B：Could I try a larger one?

我可以試穿大一點的嗎？

類似用法

例 Can I try a smaller one?
我能試穿較小件的嗎？

例 Do you have this color in size 8?
這個顏色有八號嗎？

例 Do you have these shoes in size 7?
有七號的鞋子嗎？

MP3 429

● 詢問試穿結果

How does this one look on me?

我穿這一件的效果怎麼樣？

> 若是你想要詢問朋友你試穿的效果好不好，可以問"What do you think?"或"How do they feel?"

A：How does this one look on me?

我穿這一件的效果怎麼樣？

B：It looks great on you.

你穿看起來不錯。

同義用法

例 Take a look for me.

幫我看一看。

相關用法

例 Where is the mirror?

鏡子在哪裡？

MP3 430

● 喜歡試穿結果

It feels fine.

我覺得不錯。

> 若是試穿的效果非常滿意，就可以說"It looks great"或"It feels fine"。

A：How do they feel?

覺得它們如何？

B：They feels fine.

我覺得不錯。

類似用法

例 It's great.

好看。

例 Not bad.

不錯。

例 It looks perfect to me.

這個我喜歡。

例 It looks OK on me.

我穿看起來不錯。

 431

● 衣物太小

The waist was a little tight.

腰部有一點緊。

> 試穿結果的說明除了「太大」（too large）或「太小」（too samll）之外，也可以說太緊（too tight）。

A：Does it fit?

合身嗎？

B：Well, the waist was a little tight.

嗯，腰部有一點緊。

同義用法

例 It really feels tight.

真的有一些緊。

例 They were just too small.
它們太小了。

例 It's too tight.
太緊了。

例 It feels tight.
感覺有點緊。

例 It was too small.
這件太小了。

例 The legs weren't long enough.
褲腳的長度不夠。

反義用法

例 They were too big.
它們太大了。

例 They seem a little big.
好像有一些大。

例 This is too loose for me.
這件對我來說太鬆了。

MP3 432

●詢問有沒有庫存
Do you have this shirt in size 8?
這件襯衫有沒有八號？

當你有另外中意的尺寸時，就可以問問
銷售人員庫存中是否有存貨。

A：Do you have this shirt in size 8?
這件襯衫有沒有八號？

B：Yes, let me take one for you.
　　有的，讓我拿一件給您。

🎧 433

●喜歡商品
I like this one.

我喜歡這一件。

表示「喜歡這件商品」的說法很多種，你可以說"I like this one"或"This one is great"。

A：How do you like it?
　　您喜歡嗎？
B：I like this one.
　　我喜歡這一件。

反義用法

📖 I don't like them.
　　我不喜歡它們。

相關用法

📖 Let me think about it for a second.
　　我想一想。

📖 I don't know.
　　我不知道耶！

MP3 434

●詢問商品售價

How much?

要賣多少錢？

> 詢問「商品售價」幾乎是最基本的萬用語：**"How much is it?"**

A：You know, that sweater is a great buy.
你知道嗎，那件毛衣真的很划算。

B：How much?
要賣多少錢？

同義用法

例 How much is this?
這個要多少錢。

例 How much does it cost?
這個要賣多少錢？

例 How much did you say?
您說要多少錢？

例 What is the price?
價錢是多少？

MP3 435

●售價太貴

I can't afford it.

我付不起。

> 若是你對售價覺得不滿意，又不願意說是因為商品太貴，就可以說這個價錢你無法負擔：**"I can't afford it."**

A：It costs seven hundred dollars plus tax.

它含稅要七千元。

B：I can't afford it.

我付不起。

類似用法

例 It's too expensive.

它太貴了。

例 So expensive?

這麼貴？

MP3 436

● 討價還價

Are there any discounts?

有沒有折扣？

> "discounts"是「商品售價打折」的意思，
> 至於可以享受到多低的折扣，則要看個人
> 議價的功力囉！

A：What do you think of the price?

您覺得價格如何？

B：Too expensive. Are there any discounts?

太貴了！有沒有折扣？

類似用法

例 Can you give me a discount?

您可以給我折扣嗎？

例 Can you make it cheaper?

可以算便宜一點嗎？

例 Can you lower the price?

可以算便宜一點嗎？

> A：Can you lower the price?
>
> 　可以算便宜一點嗎？
>
> B：What price range are you looking for?
>
> 　您想要多少錢？

MP3 437

● 要求降價

Can you give me a 10 percent discount?

能給我九折嗎？

> 議價的技巧非常重要，若是你有特定的議價空間，不妨直接告訴銷售人員打個九折（**10 percent discount**）吧！

A：What price range do you want?

您心裡預算多少錢？

B：Can you give me a 10 percent discount?

能給我九折嗎？

相關用法

例 Can you lower it two hundred?

可以便宜兩百元嗎？

例 How about five thousand dollars?

可以算五千元嗎？

●合購議價

Is there a discount for two?

買兩件可以有折扣吧？

有的時候買一送一或同時買兩件也是個不錯的議價技巧。

A：Is there a discount for two?

買兩件可以有折扣吧？

B：But you have to pay it by cash.

可是您要付現金。

類似用法

例 Can you give me a discount if I buy two sweaters?

如果我買兩件毛衣，您可以給我折扣嗎？

●決定購買

I'll buy this one.

我要買這一件。

當你決定要購買商品，不妨說"I'll take it"或"I'll buy this one"。

A：Would you like to buy it?

您要買嗎？

B：Yes. I'll buy this one.

要啊！我要買這一件。

同義用法

例 I'll take them.
我要買他們。

例 I'll take it.
我要買它。

例 I'll get this one.
我要買這一件。

相關用法

例 I want both of them.
我兩件都要。

例 I want two of these.
我要買這兩件。

反義用法

例 I will pass this time.
我這次不買。

例 Not for this time.
這次先不要（買）。

 440

●要求包裝
Could you wrap it up for me?
您能幫我打包嗎？

包裝對禮品的採購來說非常重要，記得一定要提醒銷售人員代為包裝（wrap it up）。

A：Could you wrap it up for me?
　　您能幫我打包嗎？

B：OK. Would you wait for a second?
　　好的。能請您稍等一下嗎？

類似用法

例 Would you wrap it as a present?
　　可以包裝成禮物嗎？

例 Would you put them in a box?
　　可以把它們放進盒子裡嗎？

MP3 441

● 計程車招呼站
Where can I take a taxi?

我可以在哪裡招到計程車？

> 「搭計程車」就叫做"take a taxi"，而不需要使用和中文「坐計程車」一樣"sit"的字眼喔！

A：Where can I take a taxi?

　　我可以在哪裡招到計程車？

B：The taxi station is right on the corner.

　　計程車招呼站就在街角。

MP3 442

● 告訴司機目的地
City Hall, please.

請到市政府。

> 上計程車後，司機會問你"where to"，此時你只要直接說出地名或地址即可。

A：Where to?

要去哪裡？

B：City Hall, please.

請到市政府。

類似用法

例 Can you get me out there?

您能不能載我去那邊？

例 Please take me to this address.

請載我到這個地址。

 443

● 指定下車地點

Let me off at the traffic light.

讓我在紅綠燈處下車。

當你要下車時，不妨說"Let me off"就可以了！

A：Let me off at the traffic light.

讓我在紅綠燈處下車。

B：Yes, sir.

好的，先生。

類似用法

例 Let me off at the third building.

讓我在第三棟大樓(前)下車。

●抵達目的地
Here you are.

到了。

到達目的地後，計程車司機就會說"Here you are"，表示「目的地到了」的意思。

A：Here you are.

到了。

B：Is this the Seattle station?

這是西雅圖車站嗎？

●車資
How much is the fare?

車資是多少？

和前面所提過的商品售價相同"How much..."也是主要的片語，只是因為這裡要特別說明的是車資，所以是問"How much is the fare?"表示「車資是多少？」

A：How much is the fare?

車資是多少？

B：Two hundred and fifty dollars.

二百五十元。

🎵 446

●搭公車的站數

How many stops is it to Seattle?

到西雅圖要幾站？

> 在人生地不熟的國外搭公車最重要的是知道何時該下車，你可以問問公車司機"How many stops is it to + 目的地"，表示「到某地還要幾站？」

A：How many stops is it to Seattle?

到西雅圖要幾站？

B：That's the sixth stop.

那是第六個站。

🎵 447

●搭哪一班公車

Which bus could I get on to Seattle?

我應該搭哪一班公車去西雅圖？

> 當你不確定搭哪一班公車時，就應該請教"Which bus could I get on to + 目的地"。

A：Which bus could I get on to Seattle?

我應該搭哪一班公車去西雅圖？

B：You can take the 265 or the 705.

您可以搭265號或705(公車)。

●公車路線
Does this bus go to City Hall?

這班公車有到市政府嗎？

記得「路是長在嘴巴上」這句俏皮語，上車前，你應該有充分的資訊知道這班公車是否有經過某個目的地"Does this bus go to + 地點。

A：Does this bus go to City Hall?

這您公車有到市政府嗎？

B：Yes, it goes to City Hall.

有的，有到市政府。

類似用法

例 Does this bus go to the railway station?

這班公車有到火車站嗎？

例 Is this the right bus to the railway station?

這是去火車站的公車嗎？

例 Does the bus stop at the railway station?

這班公車有在火車站靠站嗎？

例 Is this bus stop for City Hall?

這個站牌有(車)到市政府嗎？

MP3 449

● 發車的頻率

How often does this bus run?

公車多久來一班？

若是你錯過上一班公車，記得要請教站
務人員，下一班公車多久才會發車。

A：How often does this bus run?

公車多久來一班？

B：About ten minutes.

大約十分鐘。

MP3 450

● 發車的時間

When will the bus depart?

公車什麼時候發車？

若是你要搭一早的公車，請確實查詢公
車發車的時間，以免太早到公車站牌等車
喔！

A：When will the bus depart?

公車什麼時候發車？

B：It starts out at 9 am.

早上九點鐘就發車了。

相關用法

例 What time is the next bus for Seattle?

下一班到西雅圖的公車是什麼時候？

●何處買公車票

Where can I buy the tickets?

哪裡可以買到車票？

> 上車前，請先買好車票喔，舉凡公車票、捷運票、火車票等，都可以用"buy the ticket"來表示。

A：Where can I buy the tickets?

哪裡可以買到車票？

B：It's over there.

就在那裡。

相關用法

例 Where can I buy a ticket to Seattle?

哪裡可以買到西雅圖的車票？

●買公車票

I'd like to buy a ticket to Seattle, please.

我要買一張到西雅圖的車票。

> "buy a ticket"是買車票的基本句型，但是請記得同時告知你是要買到哪裡（to + 某地）的公車車票喔！

A：I'd like to buy a ticket to Seattle, please.

我要買一張到西雅圖的車票。

B：Fifty dollars.

五十元。

相關用法

例 A round-trip ticket to Seattle, please.

一張到西雅圖的來回票。

例 A one-way ticket to Seattle, please.

一張到西雅圖的單程車票。

例 To Seattle for one adult and one child, please.

請給我一張大人、一張小孩到西雅圖的票。

例 Two tickets to Seattle, adult.

兩張到西雅圖的票,要成人票。

 453

●搭公車的時程
How long is the ride?

這一趟車程要多久?

搭車的資訊除了票價、目的地之外,搭車所花費的車程時間長短也是很重要的。「一段車程」就叫做"a ride"。

A : How long is the ride?

這一趟車程要多久?

B : It will take about twenty minutes.

大約需要二十分鐘。

類似用法

例 How long does it take to get there?

到那裡要多久的時間?

例 How long does this bus trip take?

坐公車要多久的時間？

相關用法

例 Is this a long ride?

車程要很長的時間嗎？

MP3 454

●在哪一站下車
Which stop should I get off at?

我應該哪一站下車？

> 「在哪一站下車」除了可以利用「第幾站下車」說明之外，也可以利用站名來判斷下車的時機。公車的「下車」是用"get off"來表示。

A：Which stop should I get off at?

我應該哪一站下車？

B：You can get off at the Seattle Hospital.

您應該在西雅圖醫院下車。

類似用法

例 Where should I get off?

我要在哪裡下車？

例 Where should I get off to go to Seattle?

到西雅圖我要在哪裡下車？

MP3 455

● 搭公車要求下車

Let me off here, please.

我要在這裡下車。

和搭計程車下車一樣,搭公車的下車也可以用"let me off"表示。

A：Let me off here, please.

我要在這裡下車。

B：Sure.

好的。

MP3 456

● 搭哪一部列車

Which line should I take for Seattle?

我應該搭哪一線去西雅圖?

火車站或捷運站中有非常多的路線,該搭哪一條路線（Which line...）,請先充分收集資料喔!

A：Which line should I take for Seattle?

我應該搭哪一線去西雅圖?

B：You can check the subway map over there.

您可以查在那裡的地鐵圖。

⑩ Which train can I take to Seattle?
我要去西雅圖應該搭哪一班列車?

⑩ Which train goes to Seattle?
哪一班車到西雅圖?

⑩ Is this the right line for Seattle?
去西雅圖是這條路線嗎?

 457

● 搭車月台

Which platform is it on?

在哪一個月台?

> 搭車月台(**platform**)是你要搭上車的地方,千萬不要弄錯月台搭錯車啊!

A : Which platform is it on?

在哪一個月台?

B : The sixth platform.

第六月台

⑩ Is this the right platform for New York?
這是出發到紐約的月台嗎?

MP3 458

● 在何處轉車

Where should I transfer to Seattle?

我要到哪裡轉車到西雅圖？

轉車和轉機一樣，都是使用"transfer"這個動詞。

A：Where should I transfer to Seattle?

我要到哪裡轉車到西雅圖？

B：When you arrive at the Maple Station, you get off and change the red line for Seattle.

當您到達楓葉車站後下車，轉搭紅線到西雅圖。

類似用法

(例) Where should I change trains for Seattle?

去西雅圖要去哪裡換車？

相關用法

(例) What train should I change to?

我要換哪一列車？

WORLD

THE BEST ENGLISH CONVERSATION FOR VACATIONS

想出國自助旅遊嗎？

不論是出境、入境、住宿，
或是觀光、交通、解決三餐，

**通通可以自己一手包辦的
「旅遊萬用手冊」**

我們有最完整的單字內容，
另外也提供您最簡便的查詢介面，
從頁面側邊即可找出您需要的單字。

**您不需要騰出大把的時間坐下來讀英文，
就讓語言能力在無形中進步吧！**

永續圖書
線上購物網

www.foreverbooks.com.tw

◆ 加入會員即享活動及會員折扣。

◆ 每月均有優惠活動，期期不同。

◆ 新加入會員三天內訂購書籍不限本數金額，

　即贈送精選書籍一本。（依網站標示為主）

專業圖書發行、書局經銷、圖書出版

永續圖書總代理：
五觀藝術出版社、培育文化、棋茵出版社、犬拓文化、讚
品文化、雅典文化、知音人文化、手藝家出版社、瓔申文
化、智學堂文化、語言鳥文化

活動期內，永續圖書將保留變更或終止該活動之權利及最終決定權。

生活句型萬用手冊

雅致風靡　典藏文化

親愛的顧客您好，感謝您購買這本書。即日起，填寫讀者回函卡寄回至本公司，我們每月將抽出一百名回函讀者，寄出精美禮物並享有生日當月購書優惠！想知道更多更即時的消息，歡迎加入"永續圖書粉絲團"您也可以選擇傳真、掃描或用本公司準備的免郵回函寄回，謝謝。

傳真電話：（02）8647-3660　　　　電子信箱：yungjiuh@ms45.hinet.net

姓名：	性別：　□男　□女
出生日期：　年　月　日	電話：
學歷：	職業：
E-mail：	
地址：□□□	
從何處購買此書：	購買金額：　　　元
購買本書動機：□封面 □書名 □排版 □內容 □作者 □偶然衝動	
你對本書的意見： 內容：□滿意□尚可□待改進　編輯：□滿意□尚可□待改進 封面：□滿意□尚可□待改進　定價：□滿意□尚可□待改進	
其他建議：	

總經銷：永續圖書有限公司

永續圖書線上購物網
www.foreverbooks.com.tw

您可以使用以下方式將回函寄回。

您的回覆，是我們進步的最大動力，謝謝。

① 使用本公司準備的免郵回函寄回。

② 傳真電話：（02）8647-3660

③ 掃描圖檔寄到電子信箱：

　 yungjiuh@ms45.hinet.net

沿此線對折後寄回，謝謝。

廣 告 回 信

基隆郵局登記證

基隆廣字第056號

雅致風靡　　典藏文化